dp

KATHA PRIZE STORIES

The best short fiction published
during 1987-1990 in ten Indian
languages, chosen by a panel of
distinguished writers and scholars.

EDITED BY
RIMLI BHATTACHARYA
GEETA DHARMARAJAN

KATHA

Rupa & Co

Published by KATHA
CII/27 Tilak Lane, New Delhi 110 001

First published, September 1991
Reprinted, November 1991

Distributed by
RUPA & CO.
15, Bankim Chatterjee Street, Calcutta 700 070
94, South Malaka, Allahabad, 211 001
P.G. Solanki Path, Lamington Road, Bombay 400 007
7/16 Ansari Road, Daryaganj, New Delhi 110 002

General Series Editor: Geeta Dharmarajan
Logo Design: Crowquill, graphic designers

Typeset in 10 on 13 pt. Palatino by dTech, New Delhi.
Made and printed in India at Ajanta Offset & Packaging Ltd., New Delhi.

ISBN 81-85586-00-4 (paperback)
ISBN 81-85586-01-2 (hardback)

CONTENTS

THE NOMINATING EDITORS

Publication of this collection has
been made possible with the
assistance of India Tourism
Development Corporation, Ltd.

PREFACE

Katha Prize Stories was originally seen as a literary magazine which would bring together through translation excellent stories (kathas), both from our country's rich oral tradition and from regional publications. The idea evoked interest but I could find no sponsors. It finally took shape as an annual anthology of stories, of which this is the first — a selection of new and noteworthy stories from the various Indian languages. The English translation you hold in your hands; a Tamil version we anticipate.

When I approached a few like-minded people, to start Katha, a registered, nonprofit organization devoted to creative communication, the idea was to encourage, foster and applaud creative writing in the various Indian languages, both for children and for adults. Using the existing publication-networks in these languages we wanted to support an active translation programme, without taking recourse to English or Hindi as a link language and without compromising on quality.

Our interest in the short story was not fuelled by some kind of misplaced sympathy to try and save a genre which has been an intrinsic part of a storyteller's repertoire in our country for many years. We knew that in many regional languages people were writing excellent stories. Only, these were not reaching beyond the four corners of their language. Out of this conviction was born Katha Vilasam, a short story research and resource centre and, this series.

When ITDC came forward with a generous grant, the Katha Awards were born. We hope that each year the Katha Awards would honour the best writing published in the regional presses, *and* the translators who have taken on the daunting job of making a story read as well in translation as it did in the original language.

Almost as soon as I started work on this project, I came upon my first hurdle. How does one, sitting in Delhi, survey the short story scene in various regions? How does one choose stories from languages which one could not even read? The questions vexed me till I finally hit upon a two-step process.

We would have a Nominating Editor for each language, some-one who not only knew his or her language and literature well, but who would actively support such a scheme. They would select three stories each from those that had been published by a quality-conscious editor in the preceding two years. The diverse tastes of editors of diverse magazines and journals (ranging from a popular commercial weekly that sells in the lakhs, to a quiet small magazine with a dedicated band of readers) could only add to the richness of the collection. We did not even *try* to represent all the Indian languages. This was determined by the writers and scholars who accepted to be our Nominating Editors.

Our Nominating Editors very readily took on the taxing job of reading as many stories as they could to finally make their three nominations. They were given a free hand to choose the stories; they, by and large, decided on the translators also. In English our Nominating Editor was requested to also look at unpublished stories. For this our first book, they have nominated some of the best stories written in the last four years, which we hope you will enjoy.

By the time the stories started coming in, I was lucky to have Rimli Bhattacharya with me, not only to coedit this collection but as director of Katha Vilasam. And, while working on this collection, we have asked ourselves many questions. Are many languages living on their past glories? Are short story writers being lured into quick money and fame by writing the serialised novel for pulp magazines? Are they being overwhelmed by 'true' stories appear-ing in regional newspapers which, through clever use of language, fantasise the real with 'support' from 'relevant' photography? Have publishers shied away from publishing short fiction because there aren't enough good stories?

The first of the Katha Award nominations brought hope with it. Many of our Editors told us that surveying the scene for this collection made them aware of the extent of excellent short stories in their respective languages. A cause for celebration, that.

But the need is still there for quality translations. The picture has not changed much since the time we started Katha. Recently, when I was in Thrissur, the headquarters of the Kerala Sahitya Akademi, I was surprised to hear that they know of no one who can go from Malayalam to Telugu (or vice versa)! And these are neighbouring languages. We need not even mention the problem of translating from, say, Manipuri or Assamese to Tamil. We feel that the need for translations is more acute today when the politics of language is putting up many narrowing walls in democratic India.

This has been a new experience for us. We have been naive. We have made mistakes. We would have been unable to bring out this book without the very sincere support given by many. This includes Shri R. K. Lakshman of ITDC who trusted us enough to agree to fund this project; our Nominating Editors who took on this labour of love, willingly; Dr Harish Trivedi who started off as our Nominating Editor for Hindi; Dr Sachidananda Mohanty, who was our Nominating Editor for Oriya but had to leave for the United States of America on a Fulbright Scholarship.

We would also like to thank Vijayalakshmi Quereshi, Meenakshi and Sujit Mukherjee, O.V. Vijayan, Urvashi Butalia, David Davidar, G.P. Deshpande, Aravind Dixit and Venkatachallam Hegde for their cooperation in our project; and Swati Mitra who helped with the editing. Not included by name here are others who have willing spent time and energy but didn't want their names mentioned. Our thanks to them is as heartfelt.

July 1991   Geeta Dharmarajan

TRANSLATING DIFFERENCES

The linguistic map of India is exciting territory in which many areas refuse to be contained within lines and with many other areas where the lines overlap, intersect and even shift. Linguistic representation alone (or more specifically, linguistic representation based on the States or all the officially recognised languages in India) is not the chief objective of this collection. The idea is to translate the richness of languages, the varying registers and the tones of the speakers and the many beliefs and desires they encode.

There has been an attempt in *Katha Prize Stories* to present the heterogeneous character of contemporary India not only through representation of different languages but by making the process of selection as many-sided as possible. However, there has always been the threat of displacement of this interesting and uneven representation by the 'homogenising' force of a single, dominant master language, English. Between the two poles lies the almost invisible criss-cross of translation. It is ironic that the more successful the crossing over, the less visible the bridges, those precarious webs of translation. *Katha Prize Stories* is really a project aimed at translating differences.

The stories in the anthology are not only from different parts of the country but are often specific to a city (Calcutta in 'The Room by the Tubewell'), a district (Rayalaseema in 'The Funeral Feast'), and even a community (the Moplah Muslims in 'Nombu'). At the risk of some confusion, we have tried to keep the original word wherever possible so that regional variations are not replaced by an 'Indian' word. For example, *Kumkum* would appear in a story whose source language belongs to the Indo-Aryan group, while stories translated from a Dravidian language would have *kumkumam* or *kumkuma*. By the same token, no regional language word has been substituted where the author has chosen to use the English — *vermilion*, as in 'Kashi.'

There is besides the inevitable question of dialect, always more challenging than the translation of standard speech. The staccatto lines in the opening section of 'The Funeral Feast' are as much the story as are the events in the story. We have found that the rhythms of colloquial speech are easier to translate from one regional language to another than to English. The first person narrator of 'The Full Moon in Winter,' the loquacious one of 'Crows, Crows and Crows' and the sparring young men in 'Maya Mriga' all have different stories to tell, but in each case the translators faced the same problem of conveying the immediacy and the fluency of spoken Marathi, Assamese and Kannada respectively.

We have always been struck by the ease with which writers in the regional languages switch to and fro between the past tense and the present tense. This is characteristic even of those stories which have sections of dialogue interspersed with sections of reported speech or internal monologue as in 'Hands,' 'The Room by the Tubewell,' or 'Nagaddhuyya.' We have tried as far as possible to retain the rhythm of the shifting tenses because they constitute some of the differences that translation aims not to erase but to make the reader aware of.

We have thought, parochially perhaps, of the Indian reader or even the subcontinental reader who is familiar or at least half familiar with many of the almost untranslatable codes, beliefs and acts of our daily lives. Therefore there is no glossary. The various words from the original language we have chosen to retain in the translation seem capable of standing on their own.

A few words have been glossed and the meaning or relevant information provided in a footnote in the belief that this information would bring alive the context of the story. For example, the meanings of *kundelu, udumu,* and *erralaka* in 'The Funeral Feast' have been given in a footnote, because it is important that the old man's fantasizing about various kinds of meat be made concrete for the reader, but inserting *hare, monitor lizard,* and *wild rat,* within the text, might draw undue attention and even defamiliarise the reader from the situation.

Primary kinship terms, like those denoting father and mother, have been retained as far as possible in their various original versions, such as *Amma, Ma, Appa, Nayana, Acchan, Abba,* and *Babuji,* since they are clearly recognisable. So too with terms expressing a secondary set of relationships where the context clarifies the meaning. Thus the little boy in 'Nombu,' calls his friend's sister *Jameelakka* rather than *Jameela sister* (which sounds contrived) or only *Jameela*, which would be contrary to the cultural code. Some words, like *Mutthassi* the Malayalam word for grandmother, in 'Prakasini's Children,' have been explicated the first time the word is used.

Another problem area is the region-specific use of an otherwise general word. In 'The Room by the Tubewell,' Hanuman Prasad, the vegetable-seller-turned-benefactor, is referred to as a *Hindustani*. Used by a Bengali in Calcutta to refer to a whole section of the migrant labour force, the word suggests both the home State of the migrants and their distinct kind of Hindi. It does not mean 'one who is from Hindustan' or more simply 'an Indian.' Both class consciousness and regionalism are embedded in this context-specific use of the word.

We wanted above all, the movement from one language to another, sometimes from one context to another to be smooth but not seamless. The seams should show, even be felt, but they should not jar and leave the reader in limbo land. To this end we have tried wherever possible to keep the rhythm of the original language, the tone and class background of the speaker and in some cases, even the distinct regionalisms. This is most evident in a story like 'Nombu' which is set in the coastal region of Karnataka. Although the characters are Saifi Moplah Muslims, they use Kannada terms instead of the Arabic or Urdu words for their prayers and in their daily speech. In 'Nombu' the Kannada word meaning fasting has been used and retained from the original title, instead of translating the word as *Roza* or *The Ramzan Fast*. The Kannada word (interestingly the same word is used by the Hindus also, as in Varalakshmi Nombu) conveys both the ritual observance of the Ramzan Fast as well as the simple fact of not having eaten, because there is no food. 'Nagaddhuyya,' the original Marathi title has been chosen over 'The Naked' which does not have the same element of ludicrousness suggested by the Marathi word.

There has been a conscious attempt to avoid using Indian words as 'local colour' but to use them frequently and unobtrusively, as they actually *are* used by most of us. Thus we have deliberately chosen not to italicise Indian words since we believe these belong and should belong to the English language as spoken and used in different parts of India.

Words like bairagi, brahmin, chami, have been capitalised only when they denote a character in a story. Thus *a* bairagi is mentioned by the narrator of 'The Curse,' but later he is *the* Bairagi who becomes a character in the story. Similarly with the brahmin priest in 'The Funeral Feast' who becomes the Brahmin or the Chami, the village sorcerer in 'Prakasini's Children.' However, honorifics such as babu, babuji, saab or forms of address as mister are not capitalised.

The translated story is double faced; even after a story has settled down in its new language, it compels us to turn and return to its land of origin. This is more than a nostalgic 'looking back' but may actually work as a historical marker. For example, the imposed and now ingrown otherness of the Partition is quite simply brought out in the pair of demonstrative pronouns of *yahan* and *wahan*. The invisible adjectives prefacing the pair are often *hamare yahan* and *unke wahan* which do not work in their clumsy literal English rendering of *our here* and *their there*. But a story such as 'Dream Images' plays constantly on the slippage between the two worlds of *yahan* and *wahan* and the unsettling movement of the adult who has ostensibly settled down in his *yahan*.

As the first tentative step of what we would like to be a long narrative, it seems premature and even presumptuous to speak of the territory covered. We could speak of areas that we have not been able to go into, of our inabilities and our own areas of darkness. The above points are only markers suggesting the direction we wish to take in our translation projects. We see this collection as an invitation for opening up of dialogues with others engaged in similar projects concerned with the issues around translation.

July 1991   Rimli Bhattacharya

MAYA MRIGA

PURNA CHANDRA TEJASVI

nominated and translated by
K. Raghavendra Rao

L ook, even a ghost must have a definite form, don't you think?'
asked Shah.

'Why must it?'

'Well, how else can it be seen by humans?'

He has a point, I thought. After all, men have access to the
external world only through one of their five senses.

'Yes, of course,' I said aloud. 'If the ghost has to be seen by *us*.'

'Okay, so we agree that it has to have a form or has to put on one
for the occasion. But, how can we be sure it's really a ghost?'

'That's simple! Suppose the ghost appeared as a pretty girl,
wouldn't that set us wondering, Why has a girl come to us at this

'*Maya Mriga*' (title of the original story) was first published in Kannada in
Kathegallu, The Kannada Sahitya Parishad, 1987.

time of the night and of all places, to a shmashana? We'll at once know that it's a ghost at work!' I said truimphantly.

'That's exactly what's bothering me. It's all our imagination . . . this stuff about ghosts appearing as boys before girls and as girls before boys! Is this a college campus or is this a shmashana? What if the ghost comes as a buffalo or a donkey?'

'But, wouldn't we still wonder why a stray buffalo has strolled into this land of the dead?'

Shah was adamant. 'No my friend, it's not that simple. Suppose the ghost appeared before you as me and were to masquerade as you before me. Then what?'

'We'll see. Let it appear first!' I said nonchalantly. Meanwhile, I had been raking up a funeral pyre with a stick.

'What the . . .!' Shah shouted. 'Why do you rake that dirty stuff?'

'What if this is a woman's corpse . . . I could well be raking up her diamond earrings or her nose ring!'

'They'd remove all that before cremating the body!' Shah retorted.

My desultory raking had brought up a few bone splinters. An imperfectly burnt corpse, I thought, and hit at the bones with my stick. Already softened by the heat they crumbled into ash.

The sky was overcast with dense dark clouds, and in the distance, the town was dimly visible by the light of the street lamps. Dassapa, our music teacher, had challenged us, 'If you have guts enough, visit the shmashana on a moonless night and you are bound to see ghosts.'

Well, we waited pretty long and saw nothing. Shah thought that he could provoke the ghosts to make an appearance if he let loose a torrent of obscenities at them. I admired his eloquence and the range of his vocabulary. But even Shah's quiver of deadly arrows eventually ran out. Exhausted, his mouth slumped into silence.

This shmashana had three platforms of stone slabs. Perhaps they had built three of them to separate the cremation sites of three different castes. Mounds of ash covered all of them. A little distance away, there was a row of graves. Bits of bones and skulls had been pushed up, probably because of fresh burials or due to the ferocious sweep of rain water.

For a while I stood silently, engrossed in our surroundings. My respect for the place rose perceptibly, this was a place to which all of us must come, all of us who have been born. But Shah was obsessed with the problem of identifying the ghost no matter in what form it might appear. Soon I too was beginning to think like him.

'Let's get out of this place before the ghosts get here looking like us,' I suggested.

'I've been thinking about it. There's one way out.'

'Well?'

'*Chumbitsam* and *Kungutsufu!*' said Shah.

I stared at him.

'That's a mantra.'

'What sort of a mantra is it? Looks like it's been made in Japan.'

'This one is made in China,' he explained. 'They are Chinese words which we are going to use as a code. As soon as I call out your name, you should first say *Chumbitsam* and then speak. When you call me, I'll first say, *Kungutsufu*. If the form that appears does not say these code words, then it's a ghost and not one of us.'

'But why Chinese words? Isn't it a better idea to use Kannada or Sanskrit?'

'No, I am now going by what our language teacher said the other day. You see, if we use our own language, it's quite likely that the ghost will understand and use it to its advantage.'

At least Shah had a plan to bail us out of a tricky situation. But I was not entirely happy about the so-called Chinese words.

Shah soon got up, announcing that he was going to take a leak. I sat there repeating the two words so that they wouldn't slip out of my mind. But as soon as I thought I had mastered my code word,

I seemed to forget the one Shah was supposed to use. When I could remember his code word my own slipped away. And when I did manage to remember both, I was confused as to which word belonged to whom! I repeated them as in a japa, as if I was repeating the divine name. How I wished we had thought of using code words from a familiar language.

Suddenly there was a noise from behind me. Probably Shah. I turned around to find him standing there. 'Hello,' I said.

'*Kungutsufu,*' he said, and then called my name. Perhaps he was rehearsing what was to be done if and when the ghost arrived. But I couldn't for the life of me recall the code word I was meant to use. Let alone the whole word, I couldn't even remember the first letter! I stared at him. Shah stared back at me. There was a hint of stiffness in his manner. Damn my memory for letting me down at such a critical juncture.

Shah waved his stick at me. He addressed me as if I were a ghost. 'You there, don't think you can fool me with your maya. I can see through you.' There was a harsh edge to his voice.

You might find all this rather funny, but believe me, it scared me to death to see Shah whirling his stick at me at that hour and in that place. I had good reason to be scared: I'd seen the village sorcerers in action exorcising spirits from those who had been possessed.

I searched desperately for that wretched word but it continued to elude me, as if I had never known it. Fear of Shah attacking me with his stick made remembering almost impossible. I gestured, asking for time to recall the word.

Shah moved a step closer. 'Out with it!' he shouted, 'Who are you really?'

God! Things were really getting out of hand. The ghosts were now reigning over both of us. If we should fall out and end up bashing out each other's brains, people would surely think that ghosts had finished us off. I must do something, fast.

Shah took another step forward.

'Please wait. Just one minute,' I blurted out, 'that wretched

Chinese word has escaped me.'

'Damn it, it's you after all!' said Shah contemptuously. He seemed disappointed that I was a mere human.

As Shah began afresh my initiation to those Chinese words, there was a pattering noise from the third pyre. A small dark cloud of smoke rose and began to take shape. It was now that our lighthearted investigations suddenly took a grim turn.

We looked at it fearfully. However, the smoke merely descended on to the ash-bed and then disappeared. We guessed that a smouldering piece of wood must have come alive and sent up the smoke-cloud, but nevertheless we went up to the pyre for a closer look.

We found a mongrel, full of eczema, asleep on the ash! It must have found such heavenly comfort in the warmth of the ash-bed that it had curled itself there, not caring to even look at us, and was now sleeping soundly like a corpse. I was sure that if it continued to sleep like that someone would sooner or later consign it to the flames.

Shah announced his decision to abandon our quest and return home. 'What kind of a shmashana is this anyway! Not even a sample ghost to be found! Let's get out of here! That music teacher probably mistook something or the other for a ghost when he was drunk.'

I was in absolute agreement. Of course, we never believed in the existence of ghosts or in their ability to appear before us. Intellectually we were atheists and rationalists, but when we found ourselves in the dark, alone with our inner selves, we turned agnostics, granting them existence.

Our music teacher had lectured to us on different kinds of veenas; the Saraswati Veena, the Rudra Veena, the Gotu Vadya and the Vichitra Veena. Finally, he came to the Kinnara Veena which was supposed to be made from a vulture's backbone. He held that if this veena was played, Mohini, a female ghost, would 'forthwith appear.' In fact, our dispute with him about ghosts began then. Who knows there may be a close link between Classical Music, Faith, Superstition and the Supernatural!

I say this because most of the musicians I know are experts in concocting tales about music to thrill their listeners. There are stories about Barkatulla Khan playing the Deepak raag on his sitar and the royal throne exploding into flames; Karim Khan singing the Malhar, and the heavens pouring forth; Alladia Khan playing the Atana raag on his sarod, and his instrument bursting into bits, and so on and so forth. There were many such fantastic tales. They did nothing for our musical interests, but drove us to search for ghosts in the land of the dead, like tantrics on an amavasya night.

When we returned to town, the Gorkha was on his rounds, striking the telegraph poles with his baton at regular intervals. He shouted a 'koun hai' when he saw us.

We felt as if we had left the world of the dead and its solemn silence to enter the familiar world of the living, and our mental alertness revived. We now spoke contemptuously about ghosts to prove to ourselves that we had not been scared in the shmashana. Ghosts might exist, but we cared nothing for them.

Suddenly Shah turned to me. 'I think ghosts do exist. But not in the shmashana.'

'Then are you suggesting that they live in towns!'

'Not there either.'

'Then?'

'In our heads, my dear Sir!'

'That's where we have our brains!'

'Correct. But ghosts do live in our heads. I came to know this only the other night. I was on my bicycle. It must have been about ten. The wind moaned as it blew through the rows of trees. Suddenly a thought struck me. Suppose a ghost was riding behind me? On the carrier? No matter how hard I tried to chase the thought away, it wouldn't leave me. As if a ghost had come out from my head. Slowly, I felt its weight settle on my carrier. It swayed this way and that, almost upsetting my balance. I was too scared to even look behind me. What if I were to find a ghost sitting there? Without turning back for a look, my body streaming sweat, I began to pedal in a trance.

'When it realised that I was not going to lose my balance, do you know what the ghost did? It reached out to me from behind and began to tickle me. It became unbearable. Tell me, mister, how could I keep cycling when something was tickling my side? I braked and jumped off my cycle.'

'What did the ghost do then?'

'The ghost? It disappeared again into my head. Vanished! Just like that. I decided to push my cycle. I was certain that if I got onto my cycle the ghost would also return from out of my head.'

Shah had really scared me by explaining at length the immense potential of the human mind. I remembered one night I was watching my image in a mirror. And I was alone. Suddenly I was terrified. Suppose my image in the mirror were to smile while I myself was not smiling? I had backed away from the mirror.

I thought that Shah's story made sense.

We were walking down one of the streets in our town. It seemed endless. I felt as if the darkness would never end and dawn never break. The only source of courage was the reassuring but dim light from the street lamps. The houses around us were in deep slumber, utterly silent. Perhaps the people inside them were all dreaming. Was I dreaming as well? Empty streets, silent houses, dishevelled-looking trees — was this all a dream?

We walked and as our bodies moved the shadows cast by them sometimes seemed to lie on the road, sometimes to stand on the walls, they'd suddenly climb up the trees and then climb down, dancing grotesquely all the while. As we watched our own shadows, we noticed a smaller shadow behind us.

'Hey, what's this?' we both said at the same time. We turned back to see an emaciated mongrel pup, full of eczema.

As soon as it saw us, it wagged its tail and shook its body briskly, letting loose a small cloud of ash which rose and merged into the wind. 'Isn't this the same animal that was sleeping in the shmashana?' Shah asked.

I shouted, 'Filthy creature, run away,' and bent down, pretending to pick up a stone. The puppy melted into the darkness.

'When did it follow us?' Shah was puzzled.

Since both of us had seen the puppy, it could not have been an illusion; of that we were certain. 'This is the work of young scamps, the rascals,' Shah raged. 'All puppies look lovely when they are little. These fellows carry the little things home, keep them for a few days, and then abandon them quite heartlessly when they pick up something like eczema. And they become stray dogs creating problems for the town.'

We walked on, talking casually, but feeling not quite comfortable. When we came to a crossing, we sensed that somebody was following us. We turned back and found the puppy right at our feet!

'Look,' I said, 'it's probably called either Tommy or Tiger. Call it by its name and chase it away.'

Shah replied, 'No, its name is neither Tommy nor Tiger. Its name is Death. That is why it was in the shmashana. We've made a big mistake bringing it back to town.'

'However that may be, it has now attached itself to us.'

'When Dharmaputra was on his way to Heaven, a dog afflicted with eczema is supposed to have followed him. This pup must be a descendent of that dog!'

I didn't quite relish such grim jokes in an empty street and so late at night. Determined to sever all connections with the puppy, I lifted it bodily and flung it into the garbage drum near the street lamp. We quickly moved away from the spot and looked back to see if the creature had started to follow us again. We saw the puppy trying to climb out of the drum and heard it yelp. We ran up to the post office hoping to give the puppy the slip. Panting for breath, we paused. We could see the puppy in the light of the street lamp. It was following us but was still about five street lamps away. By now we were convinced that it was impossible either to scare it away or to escape it by running away ourselves.

'It was a mistake to have gone to the shmashana in the first place,' I began to mumble. 'Now we should consider ourselves lucky if we can get rid of this creature.'

'Perhaps it was a ghost sleeping on the pyre in the form of an eczema-stricken puppy.'

I was bored by the whole thing. 'Look mister, this sort of thing may work well as symbols in modernist short stories, but this is not Death, nor is it any ghost. It's just a puppy. It is in need of a master who can feed it and that's why it is following us. Please think of a way to get rid of it. Look at its face! Can it really be called a puppy? Looks more like a fox — a cross between a dog and a fox!'

'Hold on. I have a solution,' said Shah as he ran after the puppy to catch it. Fearing that he would throw it back again into the garbage drum, the puppy ran a fair distance away from him. But as soon as we moved on, it began to follow us. When Shah tried to catch it, it again eluded him.

Failing repeatedly to catch it and quite exhausted by his efforts, Shah said angrily, 'Look, mister, it *is* Death. This I guarantee. I am positive it is the ghost from the shmashana — I shall give it to you in writing if you like. It has taken the form of a diseased puppy, realising that there is danger if it approaches us as a pretty girl.'

Shah changed his strategy. Instead of chasing the puppy, he snapped his fingers to coax it closer to him. Taken in by Shah's display of affection, the little animal came near him. Swiftly, Shah lifted it by the folds of the skin around its neck, and then dumped it with considerable force into a nearby house. This was the only house with a compound and he dropped it inside without making the slightest noise. He was then free of it. We were relieved and happy. Shani, the deity of ill-omen who seemed to have overtaken us, had been transferred to someone else.

We had hardly gone four steps when the wretched pup began to yelp, almost rhythmically, from within the compound. We heard a gruff voice shout, 'Shoo! Shoo!' from inside the house. We moved a little distance away into the obscurity of the darkness and waited. The pup continued to cry as if singing a bhajan. The lights inside the house came on. A human being with a hirsute body like a bear lumbered out, still swaying under the spell of sleep. He lifted the pup which sat wailing near his door, and threw it outside the compound as if it was a piece of dirt. Then he disappeared into the house as suddenly as he had appeared.

The lights went off inside the house. The puppy ran towards us and began wagging its tail. What else could we do but stare at each other?

'Who is that fellow?'

Shah answered, 'He must be an agent of Yama, the God of Death. Whoever he is, I'm going to have some fun.'

He took the puppy back to the house and dropped it inside once again. Then he ran back into the cover of the darkness.

Once again we heard the same gruff voice roar. The man flung the puppy out, but did not forget to keep the gate open before he went inside probably cursing the fact that his house had a compound.

The puppy was back with us.

'It is indeed Death,' Shah said. 'You should know this by now, my friend.'

Once again, he lifted the pup and went back to the same house. He shut the gate, dropped the pup inside and then ran back to our hiding place.

I was quite upset. How could Shah who had been gentle and full of light-hearted fun only this morning, now indulge in such a cruel game. But curiosity as to what would happen next rooted me to the spot.

Once again we heard the puppy cry. The hairy bear-man completely lost his patience. He flung open the doors. When we saw him come out of the house with a huge club, our strength gave way. He opened the gate with a thunderous noise. The poor puppy which was lurking nearby, managed to slip past the man and attached itself to us like a shadow. The bear-man went around the house swinging his club. I hoped fervently that he would soon go back into the house. But we saw him pause near the gate.

Perhaps he too suspected that it was all the work of a ghost. Perhaps he had further doubts. Perhaps he was unwilling to believe in ghosts. Perhaps he was calculating that there was human design behind what had been happening. He shut the gate, but this time, instead of going inside again, he rested his head against the gate, waiting.

Death was before us in the darkness, itself becoming part of the darkness, wagging its tail.

We stood still like statues and dared not move. We knew that even if he got the slightest hint of our presence, the bear-man would bash our brains out. We were like corpses trapped in a tomb, immobile in the shadows. But for how long could one stand like that! Supposing the bear-man was prepared to wait the whole night . . . .

I cursed Shah in a whisper. 'It's all because of you. You've got us into this mess!'

Shah became defensive. 'How can you accuse me? It is all the work of this ghost here. Wasn't it your idea that we must somehow get rid of it? Let's wait and see how long he can keep the vigil. After all, he'd want to sleep too, wouldn't he?'

We stood motionless, waiting for that bear wrapped in a dhoti to go away. We waited quite long, but the fellow continued to stand there, equally motionless. We wondered if we should run away even while he stood there. But supposing the bear-man could run faster than us — one blow from his club would be enough to send us back to the shmashana.

Shah was ridden with doubts about the man. He said, 'Looks like he has fallen asleep standing there at the gate. How else can a human being stand motionless this long?'

I was at a loss about our next move. My legs had begun to ache with the long hours of standing. The puppy too must have got fed up, or perhaps it rated the bear-man higher than it did us, or perhaps it wanted to let the man know that we were standing there. Whatever the reason, the puppy turned round, and moved slowly towards him. We were so scared that we didn't know whether we should flee the scene or stay on.

We stood there imagining how the bear-man would send the puppy to the land of Yama with a single blow of his club.

The puppy went and stood in front of him. His body which appeared to be asleep, showed no signs of movement. We heard the sound of the club falling from his hand. All of a sudden the gate opened and his body fell with a thud along the stone slab near the door. Death the puppy easily went past the body and, unobstructed, entered the house.

God knows whether the fellow was asleep, had fallen unconscious, or had just died.

Before the people inside the house chased the puppy out, before that ghost from the land of the dead started to follow us again, before dawn broke, we had to run away.

We both ran for our lives, leaping out of that darkness, our hearts filled with the fear of death.

CROWS, CROWS AND CROWS

BHUPENDRANARAYAN BHATTACHARYYA

nominated by Indira Goswami
translated by Ranjita Biswas

It was dusk. A man sat in a corner of Bruta Garden. He was carving out a watermelon with a sharp knife and eating it with evident relish as he watched people drift by, when a young man wearing dark glasses stopped and asked for a match in rather elaborate gestures.

The older man waved his piece of watermelon at him impatiently. I'm busy, he seemed to say. Try further ahead.

The stranger suddenly turned militant. 'You!' he sneered. 'I've met many like you. Quite the gentleman in looks, aren't you? People like you only lack basic courtesy. Boor! Did I ask you for your bed to sleep on? All I wanted was a matchstick. Damn it! You

'*Kauri, Kauri, aru Kauri*' ('Crows, Crows and Crows') was first published in Assamese in *Sutradhar*, September 16-30, 1990.

can keep your matches.'

The man hadn't bargained for such a show of temper. It was only after the youth had harangued, kicked violently at the grass, and then started to stalk away that the man stopped chewing. He clicked his tongue awkwardly to draw attention. Then he stood up and shouted, 'Hey, mister!'

The youth came back to stand right before him.

'Why are you so angry? Here!'

The youth took the matchbox but when he drew out his cigarette packet, it was empty. He crumpled it into a ball and threw it away.

'Sorry, sir!' he said sheepishly. 'The squabble was unnecessary. Please excuse me. I didn't know I was going around with an empty pack. I forgot that we'd finished all the cigarettes in the office.'

'That's all right. It has happened to me so many times. Quite often an empty pack remains on my table for days and then I forget and offer cigarettes to my visitors. It's embarrassing when they say it's empty!'

'I know. Still, I should have noticed it earlier.'

'Now come, forget it and have a smoke. I won't smoke now. First attend to hunger then think of other addictions — that's what I believe. In any case, I hardly smoke.'

The youth took a cigarette and lit it.

The sun was almost gone. The leaves on the trees had taken on a yellowish tinge. The road outside was gradually getting crowded. Suddenly, they saw the Prime Minister's car pass by.

The youth looked in the direction of the car with a sardonic smile on his face.

'The PM looks healthier these days,' he remarked maliciously as he returned the cigarette packet and the matchbox. 'Not so long ago he looked like me.'

The man smiled absentmindedly and continued to devour his watermelon. 'But the PM can't beat me,' he said. 'I'm fairer!'

'Yes, that you are,' the other agreed, 'you're a handsome chap all right. The colour of gold, too! But I'm in a foul mood today and in no state to laugh. Actually, I had a fight with my Boss. I was too upset to even have lunch.'

'What do you do? Where do you work?'

'Public relations. In a private company.'

'If you haven't had lunch, why don't you have some of this watermelon? I always have fruits for lunch — from April to September. Fruits are so cheap in Delhi!' The youth had finished his cigarette by then. 'Have some? I assure you I've not used my teeth on them!'

The man cut out a third of the remaining watermelon.

'I find these things too bland. Besides, I don't like fruits. But if you insist . . . .'

'Did you come to blows with your Boss?'

'No, I didn't! But I'm still very angry at his behaviour. He doesn't like me. What's the point in working with someone who doesn't like you?' the youth asked as he worked his way through the watermelon.

'Did he behave badly with you?'

'*Yes!* Perhaps I haven't been able to make you understand. Actually, it happened like this. This morning I suddenly remembered my mother . . . .'

'Where's your hometown?'

'It's quite near. Agra.'

'Well?'

'I thought why not skip office today and visit my mother; tomorrow I'll tell the Director that I had been down with high fever. On the way to the Inter-State Bus Terminal, I dropped in at a sweet shop to buy some mithai for my mother. And there at the counter, I suddenly saw the Director's face in the mirror. He was standing just behind me. I suppose it always happens like this. What you fear most will always take place. I lost all my enthusiasm when I saw him and turned my face away. But he wouldn't leave me alone. Why, Achintya! It is almost eleven o'clock! he said. I didn't like his sarcastic tone and made up a story on the spot. Sir, I got up late this morning. It was cloudy, you see. I didn't have the time to make rotis. So I thought of eating something here before going to work. He flashed a smile at me. His seeming cordiality unnerved me completely! After all, anything can happen in a private company — though, of course, the Union in our office is very strong. But that doesn't help me, does it? My relationship with the Union Secretary isn't exactly cordial.

'Ultimately, I abandoned the idea of visiting my mother and got into a 33 number bus to go to office. All the way I was disturbed by thoughts of my mother. Once inside my room, I didn't feel like doing any work; I put my legs up on the table feeling thoroughly frustrated. At one point I even thought of asking the Director for leave but then I changed my mind.'

'Why does the Director dislike you so much?' the older man asked, pointblank.

'I don't know.'

'There must be a reason.'

'Well, I'm not sure. People tell me I get on his nerves. I don't know why. Do I look so obnoxious?'

'How would I know, brother, that's your problem.'

'I think I know the reason. Unlike the others I don't go into his room often enough to flatter him. Their praises are of course only lies. Most of them don't do any work. They just park themselves in his room and indulge in endless adda. Every hour or two they send someone out to bring paan and zarda and then chew on the stuff like goats. I find the whole thing quite insufferable.'

'But what happened *today*?'

'Ha! After some time, our Union Secretary came to my room and asked me why I tend to *keep ruminating* like this everyday in the office. I've disliked the fellow for a long time and this was my chance to get even. Give me my bonus and I'll be happy, I told him. He laughed sarcastically: Is it the bonus or something else? My blood boiled at his words for he knew how angry I was. He guffawed shamelessly and went out of the room, still smoking the cigarette I had given him. I shouted at his departing figure, Shall we get the bonus by the end of the month? He gave a noncommittal reply. Furious, I called him the pet dog of the Director! But the bastard only smirked. He came back after ten minutes as if paying me a courtesy call and offered me a cigarette. Then he brought out a pen and wrote something on a piece of paper. I didn't see what he was writing, and frankly, I didn't care. I grabbed this opportunity to remind him about the Diwali bonus — though not in a very civilised manner. He looked daggers at me. I retaliated by bombarding him with all the choice gaalis I knew. He couldn't take this for long and went out of my room slamming the door behind him. To make a point, I kicked at the door too. It was just as well that he'd left. I was feeling terribly violent and was quite ready to beat him up. But after he'd gone, my mother's face came back to me. I felt like running away from the office. How I wished a minister or someone important had died — at least it would have ensured a half-day off — and I could have gone and seen my mother without any problems.'

There was silence after this long account.

The youth drew closer. 'Do you know what happened then? As if it was all waiting to happen to me. There is a steel almirah in one corner of my room. And behind it there is a basket full of old papers — I had completely forgotten about it. Suddenly, I heard the sound of birds. I tried to guess where it came from. At first, I didn't see anything. But then I seemed to glimpse a cat's tail. Yes! It was a cat, staring at me from near the door. I had never seen cats in the office — How did one get in here today? I was bored. I didn't want to work. I didn't know how to while away the time either. So I amused myself by staring at the cat's eyes, and she looked back with her hunter's eyes. As I went on observing her, it seemed that the cat was ridiculing me. Thoroughly irritated, I crumpled a piece of paper and threw it at the cat. She miaowed and fled. All this time, I'd been hearing the harsh cry of crows but I hadn't found it unusual. Now gradually the cawing seemed to rise to a crescendo. Hundreds of crows had surrounded the building and the air resounded with their unpleasant cry. A feeling of irritation and uneasiness overtook me. I got up to see what was happening.

'I was about to leave the room when I got a shock. A crow flew in through the window and perched itself on my table. Turning its neck this way and that as if looking for something, its claws scratched the table. I found this very unnerving. Why had the crow come to my table today? I was scared and wondered why I should feel so. I came out to the balcony and looked down at the Director's room. A crowd had gathered outside the room. The Director himself was surrounded by his stenographer and a few officers. His peon was explaining in a loud voice that somebody had just destroyed the crows' nest which had been in the hollow of a nearby tree for god knows how long. That was why the crows were creating such a ruckus. The Director went back to his room with the steno. He must have been in the middle of dictating something. After a while the computer operator and the programmer went in too. But the noise outside only increased, and more crows joined in. The chowkidar threw stones at them but after a brief silence the crows started again with greater enthusiasm. The Director came out looking visibly irritated. The others too looked irritated. Then he appeared to smile. The others immediately tried to smile in unison. The Director said he could never have imagined that there was a large nest outside his room. His companions agreed readily. But the Boss seemed annoyed at such sycophancy. He called for the chowkidar. The latter came in looking apprehensive. What have you been doing? If you continue like this, you'll soon be out of a job, the Director barked. The scared chowkidar stood there with his head bowed, looking like a convict. Then an officer came and tried to remove the nest. Immediately, a crow swooped down and tore away quite a bit of his hair. The officer fled in utter panic. The others scattered here and there.'

'And then?'

'What do you expect? Another officer tried to muster up enough courage to throw away the nest. Why do you think they were so eager to oblige? To impress the Director, of course. But when somebody remarked that the crows might pluck out his eyes, the officer hesitated.'

'Where were you all that time?'

'On the second floor balcony.'

'What happened then? Isn't there anybody else in your room?'

'There are five others. But all five have gone on deputation for a computer training course. So I've been all alone for the past one month. I came back to my room, stretched my legs on the table and decided to enjoy my cigarette. Somehow I felt lonely; my mother's face cut through my thoughts again and again. As I smoked, I once again heard the scratching sound from behind the almirah. This time I immediately went over to the narrow space leading to the back of the almirah. I was shocked by what I found. I wondered how it could have happened.'

'What?'

'I saw three fledglings! Their wings had not yet grown; probably they were not even a week old. Certainly, they could not fly. Perhaps, after their nest was broken their mother had somehow placed them on my window sill. They must have hopped little by little to take shelter in the wastepaper basket, or perhaps the mother herself had carried them to safety there. There were various possibilities, but how the birds got there was still a mystery. However that may be, I was now more interested in taking advantage of the situation. A wicked idea came to my mind: Suppose I threw one of the birdies straight down, it would fall near the Director's room. Hundreds of crows were sure to surround it immediately! I also knew if I threw a bird from this height, it was bound to die immediately. And that's exactly what happened. The bird started vomitting blood. Slowly the spot where it had fallen was invaded by innumerable crows. The lawn near the Director's room turned black with birds.'

'And you kept standing?'

'No, no! I didn't take the risk of making anyone suspicious.'

'Where did you go?'

'To the canteen. I saw the Union Secretary there having a discussion with some colleagues. I went up to him. How can we work like this? The crows have completely ruined my mood. Let us go and ask for a half-holiday, I said.'

'What was his reaction?'

'It's difficult to make him out. When I suggested the half-holiday, he laughed so loudly I thought the roof would fall. What do you intend doing with your half-holiday? he asked. I hated his tone. That's none of your business, I told him. He hadn't expected this. He took time formulating his next strategy. What a good idea! he said bitingly. WORKERS AGITATE ON ACCOUNT OF CROWS! An interesting piece for tomorrow's newspaper. Do you want to create such an incident just to get noticed? Do something that has never happened before? Do you want to make history? he asked. His way of putting things made the others cackle with laughter.

'I was disgusted. I came away to find out what was happening. As I approached the dead crow, I got a glimpse of the Director from behind the curtain. He looked very flustered — as though he would like to resign immediately. He walked past me, his shoes making a staccato sound, and as soon as he had got into his car, he rolled up the glass. The steno ran after him with the papers and got in beside him. From the opposite direction came Mehta — he seemed interested in knowing why the Director was cooped up inside the car. Why is he dictating to the steno in that soundproof car? he mumbled and without waiting for an answer he quickly walked away.

I was pretty disappointed that my efforts had been of no use. I took out my file to finish some pending work. But I just couldn't concentrate. I felt as if there was no meaning to life; the world had become a joyless prison. Still, hoping for god knows what, I flung the other two birdies on the car, thinking they'd be killed instantly. I quickly moved away from there pretending to be busy. I was worried that somebody might have seen me. But, I couldn't sit back for long. I wanted to see the result of my efforts. From the balcony I saw that the Director's white Maruti was surrounded by hundreds of crows. The little birds were still alive. I saw the car pulling out from the compound. I felt happy at last. It seemed certain that the Director was not coming back today! Now that the Boss was out, what was there to keep me in office. I pushed off. But I'm worried, I can tell you. What if someone had seen me and thinks of informing the Director!'

'Suppose I do?' teased the older man.

The youth smiled.

Just then a fruitseller went by with a basket of grapes. The older man called out to him and began enquiring about the price.

'Okay then! I'll be on my way. I can still catch the Delhi-Agra passenger train. It will only take four hours to get there. I'll come back tomorrow morning in time for office.'

'Won't you have some grapes?'

'No, I told you I don't like fruits. I think I should be off.'

'Okay then! We'll meet again sometime.'

'I hope you haven't been offended by my behaviour. Please forgive me,' repeated the youth as he departed.

The man plucked a grape from the bunch and tasted it to see whether it was sweet or sour. When he made up his mind, he asked for 250 grams. The vendor made up the packet.

The man let out a shriek as he put his hand into his pocket. He started muttering to himself, and then said aloud, 'I've been duped!'

The fruitseller got up.

Some others had also gathered.

'I was suspicious,' the fruitseller declared.

'What made you suspicious?'

'When the Crow stood up and went off . . . .'

'Crow? What Crow are you talking about?'

'We know him as the Crow — that one who sat chatting with

you. Don't you understand, Saheb?'

'No, I don't understand anything.'

'He's a pickpocket. Most of us vendors know him only by that name.'

'No, he's a public relations officer in a company.'

'Did you ask him which company?'

'No, I didn't.'

'That's the story he tells everyone. Did he start off by asking you for a match?'

'Yes, he did.'

'Did he have an empty cigarette packet?'

'Yes, that's right.'

'Then, you can be sure. He's the one who stole your purse.'

'Do you know where he lives?'

'Sorry, Saheb. I only know him as the Crow. Nothing more. Anyway, you can't catch him.'

'Why?'

'Do you have any proof that he stole your money?'

'No, I don't. All I have are my suspicions.'

'If someone sits next to you, how can you assume that he is the Crow?'

'True enough.'

'But he stole the purse — that's for sure,' the fruitseller concluded.

THE FUNERAL FEAST

SWAMI

nominated and translated by
Vakati Panduranga Rao

It was the hour for food. The hour when a ball of rice has to go in to put out that gnawing hunger in the pit of the stomach.

The sun was burning like a fireball.

Not a single leaf dared to move. It was hot and humid. Sweltering heat and stifling humidity. The sky was clear. Not a single cloud in sight. Not a drop of rain. People lived . . . eating a tuber here, a wild plant there. But how did the cattle manage? •

Famine.

Dearth of grains.

Dearth of grass.

Sun, the hot rapacious sun.

'Saavu Koodu' ('The Funeral Feast') was first published in Telugu in the *Andhra Prabha Illustrated Weekly*, October 18, 1989.

Heat inside the house and outside.

Crickets screeching from the bushes.

Kites soaring overhead.

The brook, like an old woman's breasts, was shrivelled and dry. The water tank was full of bandicoot-burrows.

Men had no work. The cooking pot had no grain.

Putting aside their hunger, boys played 'tiger and goat' with pebbles on the bund. If they wore a shirt, they were naked below the waist; if they happened to wear knickers, they had no shirt above. Shame was a luxury for women whose torn blouses exposed their armpits and breasts. Women were ready to sleep with any-body for a bundle of grass. How could anyone in such a village even think of a full meal?

Three years since the rains had come.

Three years since the crops had grown.

Three years and not a loan repaid.

Three years and not a daughter married.

Sun, sun and more sun. Heat, heat and more heat.

Lighting a bidi; chewing a dry betel leaf . . . what else was one to do? No work, no festivals even; how was one to spend time? Under the trees, on the tilted bullock carts, on the bund — all over the village they dozed, their knees folded into their stomachs.

Dead.

The old man who had been neither fully alive nor fully dead for the last ten days was now dead. He lay on an urea-plastic sheet, he who had managed to survive for ten days on a few drops of his wife's diluted coffee each day.

'You there, Pedda-Appayya is dead.'

Rearranging their paibattas over their shoulders, the men moved in like corpses.

Death. Well, death visits everyone. So it did Pedda. In times such as this, one is better dead than alive. Hard times, when two rupees will barely get you two seers of ragi. When it is difficult to get a seer of jonnalu for two rupees and a half. And dry chillies are selling at sixty rupees a kilo. Ayyo! Not even two seers of salt for a rupee? What rotten times are these!

With prices soaring so high, why bother trying to keep alive? Who was to know what worse times lay ahead? Blessed were those who had not waited to see such days. The old man was certainly lucky to die. It was his misfortune that he had to die with his last desire unfulfilled.

Pedda had slogged like a bullock all his life. He had survived on starch-water but had managed to bring up his three sons, get them married, and when all of them went their own ways, he did not owe a single paisa to anybody. He had earned the respect of the whole village. And yet, an old man such as this died with his last desire unfulfilled.

Did he have sons?

Yes, he did.

Were there no relatives?

Yes, yes, they were very much there.

There were sons and relatives, but in times such as these, every one has to fend for himself and who can care for the next man, even if he is your father? Poor Pedda! He died with his last desire unfulfilled.

The old man had been living with his youngest son. A month ago he had fallen ill and his eldest son, Mareppa, had come to see him and he'd asked, 'Nayana, how are you?'

'Son, I may not live for many days.'

The son was pained by his father's words. 'Don't speak so,' he said.

'I speak the truth. Only I know the agony of my body.'

The old man's eyes were wet.

There are some who fly to America when they run the slightest temperature and here was someone who did not have money to go to the next village to get an injection. One might perhaps think of money or the lack of it if it were a young man. But, the old fellow is bound to die tomorrow if not today; how can one think of injections and tonics for him? Especially now when everyone is starving. Buying medicines to save an old life?

The old man whispered, 'Son, it's ages since I've had some toddy. I feel like having a pot or two. Let me have four rupees.'

The eldest son did not reply immediately. Four rupees meant a day's food, or salt and chillies for three days.

The son's silence sank deep into the old man and rose to his throat choking him.

After a while he said, 'Son, I will not live for many days. Let me have toddy just this once before I die. I will not live long enough to be able to ask you for money again. If there is no joy in living, can there be meaning in life? So let me drink just once and die happily. That's all.'

With his father repeatedly talking of death, Mareppa had no option but to take out four rupees from his banian pocket and give it to the old man.

And Mareppa got it from his wife for shelling out the four rupees to his father.

The youngest son got an extra five acres written in his name by promising that he would look after the old couple in their last days. The old man should have asked *him* for the money. Why did he have to ask *you*? If he had given the land to us we would have certainly looked after him now. But no, those two old people never had any love for us or any faith that we would care for them. Fine! Then, how dare he ask you for four rupees today? Even if he were shameless enough to ask you, you should've had more sense than to give away the money just like that! She was in a frenzy. She screamed at her husband, tore the old man to pieces and spat fire on her younger brother-in-law.

At the end of what seemed to Mareppa an endless bout of cursing and screeching, she took her children into her arms and broke into a wail. 'Why don't you go ahead and kill me and my kids? You are Daata Karna, aren't you, giving away everything? Why should you bother about your wife and children? My lord, look at our torn clothes, at our sunken bellies and protruding bones. If we eat for a day we starve for a week, but does that bother you? No! You are a noble lord who showers money on every stranger on the street. Tell me Almighty God, how am I to give a morsel of food to my children and keep them alive with such a feckless creature for a husband?'

She went on and on till the sun had set. But the old man who was on his deathbed sat up, revived after the mandatory two pots of toddy.

'It's a solid heart that the old fellow has inside him,' joked the villagers.

'What a fool I was to have given those four rupees, thinking that the old man would die,' lamented Mareppa.

Within a week, the old man was taken ill again.

His second son Naganna, came to see him. Sitting at one end of the cot he inquired about the old man's health.

'I'm finished, son,' sighed the old man.

Father and son talked for a while.

Desire. Desire began hissing inside the old man, but he was shy of expressing it. He knew that his second son was not in a position to fulfil his desire. But perhaps he was prepared to beg, borrow or steal to satisfy his father's last wish.

'Naganna!' the old man called out.

'Yes, Nayana.' Naganna came closer.

'Nothing.' The old man sighed deeply.

Naganna's situation was extremely wretched. Knowing this, the old man could not tell him what he wanted. He had distributed his land, five acres each, to his three sons. Each had to work his field with his family to keep body and soul together. But for the past three years not even the grain last sown had returned home. Even the wetlands around the pond had ceased to offer a livelihood to the labourers. Things were so bad, that many had migrated to Bellary the past year looking for work in the cotton fields. Naganna's wife had run away with someone during this time. She could not be blamed. She had long suffered from a terrible pain in her stomach and despite her pleas, Naganna had not taken her to a doctor, for he had no money. So when a man came along promising to do so, she ran away with him, not hesitating for a moment to leave her husband and children behind. Since that day, Naganna's eldest daughter had been cooking the daily gruel.

Naganna stood up. 'I must go. I have to take the bullocks to water.'

Desire. A burning desire. A last wish. Would he or wouldn't he? What is the harm in asking once.

'Naganna.'

'Yes, Nayana.'

'I feel like eating mutton-rice.'

'Mutton! When do we ever get to eat mutton these days? The last time we had mutton was when we sacrificed the goat at the Maremma festival. Not a goat has been killed in the past six months. How can we get mutton, Nayana? Why mutton, Nayana? Since we sold off all the chickens, you can ransack the village and not find an egg anywhere.'

Naganna could not bear to look at his father's face. He left.

One should have seen Pedda Appayya when he was young. He was a man who could polish off two full meals and get ready for the third even before his hands were dry. The first day his wife cooked for them after their marriage, she made three big balls of rice and served them with some pickle. She placed the food between them and thought that he would eat two and she could eat the third. He came in after washing his face and hands. His wife placed one big ball of rice in his hands. He ate it up. She served him the second, he ate that up as well. She thought he would now get up to wash his hands. But no, he didn't. He finished the third big ball of rice and she slept on an empty stomach.

The following day she cooked some more rice and made four big balls. She hoped that he would eat three and she could eat one. When he had finished the first three she thought he would say, No to the fourth. But Appayya ate that too and the wife went hungry again. On the third day, she made six balls of rice. She served him all six balls of rice and he was more than a match to the challenge. She had expected that he would jump up and go away at the sight of the sixth ball but there he was, looking shyly at her and eating the sixth as well.

That was it. She ran away to her mother's house. She clung to her mother and she wailed, 'Amma, what sort of a man have you got me for a husband, I'm like a widow. The man does not have a stomach, it is a bottomless pit that he has. How can I live with someone who starves me day after day?'

The village elders called a panchayat meeting and Appayya was asked, 'It seems that you are starving your wife, is it true?'

A bewildered Appayya answered, 'I don't know . . . she served me food and I ate it. I never told her not to eat . . .'

'No, he never forbade me to eat, but what am I to eat when he licks off the last grain from the pot?'

One of the elders advised Appayya. 'Look here young man, you should first find out how many balls of rice there are in the pot. You cannot sit before the pot expecting your wife to ask you to get up. We are children of perpetual starvation, so all the rice in the world will not suffice to meet our hunger. We are not stinking rich Kuberas to eat our fill. If you cannot learn to say No to food now, how are you going to look after your wife? How will you raise children later?'

Such was the extent of Pedda Appayya's appetite. He was full of contempt for the poor chaps who could not stir out to work without a cup of coffee in the morning. As for him, he could work for hours together on an empty stomach, provided he had enough food on his return.

He could not ask his eldest son for mutton. His eldest daughter-in-law had kicked up such a fuss over the four rupees that her husband had given him for his toddy.

His second son had had to refuse him.

The third son had six daughters, all very young. He and his wife slaved all day to feed them. Because the fellow had so many mouths to feed, he had been given an extra five acres and also the house. This had been resented by the other two sons.

If he had the money, the second son would have taken his father to the hospital. But he who could not even buy a capsule when the old man fell ill, how could he now provide mutton curry?

The old man remained silent.

But Pedda Appayya could not get rid of his obsession for the taste of mutton. He thought constantly of the many ways in which it could be cooked and enjoyed. Roasted, with a pinch of salt . . . . Boiled . . . . Whoever came to see him, in what they thought were his last days, was given a lecture on the relative merits of different kinds of meat. 'Kundelu* . . . well, no; that gives you gas. But the udumu*, now. *That* makes a good curry. It also gets rid of pain. The erralaka* is tasty, but it does have an obnoxious smell . . . .'

The whole village laughed behind his back, 'The old man is on his death bed and listen to him drool over meat!'

Dead.

He who was constantly dreaming of mutton curry was dead at last. The sons came with their wives and children. All the relatives arrived. There were many others too who appeared. The women wailed. The children stood around, gaping.

The sons were trying to arrange for the burial. The list of essential items was long: vermilion, turmeric powder, incense sticks, saffron, bamboo poles and rope to make the 'last-stretcher.' One can get along in life without many things but it is not so in

In order of appearance, the asterisked words refer to the hare, the monitor lizard and the wild rat.

death; all these things had to be got, and immediately.

'Mareppa, have you sent for udukaddilu?'

'Naganna, why don't you go to the shop and get some sambraani?'

'Obulesu, did you get the kumkuma that I'd asked for?'

'We need pasupu immediately, Anna.'

Everyone was shouting instructions and nothing was getting done. Nobody was prepared to spend a single paisa of his own. Many an item was talked about but nothing was to be seen. Time was running out; each of the three brothers hoped that the other would pay for the funeral.

The elders of the village understood their predicament. They got together all the three sons and told them, 'Now look, one of you must take on the entire responsibility and bear all the expenses. Spend as much as is required until all the ceremonies are over and keep an account. Add up everything and then share the burden equally.'

The eldest son agreed to bear the expenses for the time being. The shopkeeper agreed to give credit. And finally things got under way.

The drumbeaters were sent for. They demanded forty rupees.

The sons were prepared for only twenty.

'All right,' said the beaters finally, 'pay thirty and we will beat the drums!'

'Thirty solid rupees for merely beating the drums? What a waste. What if the drums are not sounded?' shouted the youngest son.

'Damn you beggars!' one of the beaters cursed them. 'Three sons a man has and now that he's dead you say you can't even arrange for the drumbeat! Were you really born to him or to someone else?'

The sons agreed to thirty rupees.

The next bit of work was to dig a pit to bury the dead man. The diggers asked for fifty rupees.

'Fifty rupees for digging a pit and that too in the soft soil near the bushes! It's far too much!' said the sons and offered twenty.

The diggers came down to forty. After considerable haggling they came down to thirty-five and refused to lower their rates any further.

Thirty-five rupees for digging a pit! For the eldest it meant a month's supply of Ganesh brand bidis which he bought in ones and twos and which he smoked only up to half the length, reserving the rest for another time. The second son saw in the thirty-five rupees his wife who had eloped for want of treatment, and the third son saw in it his youngest daughter running around naked for want of clothes.

By dusk the body was buried.

On their way home they stopped to consult the Brahmin in the Aanjaneyaswami temple. The tenth day happened to fall on a Ashtami. It was decided that the final ceremony and dinner would be held on the eleventh day.

Mareppa, the eldest son, went to the shepherd and picked out from the flock an aged and withered sheep. The animal was anaemic and hardly able to walk — it was just like the old man before his death. They would have liked a fat young sheep but that would have meant five or six hundred rupees. Who had that kind of money?

They killed the animal on the tenth day, after midnight. Its blood was collected in a pot. The head was severed and roasted. The odds and ends were tried out raw by some among those who had gathered there. The peculiar greasy odour emanating from the burning wool tickled the tastebuds of those who were not able to take part in the preparations of the feast.

The legs were cut off and tossed into the fire. The animal was skinned; then the belly was slit open and the intestines taken out, the faeces were removed and the entrails cleaned with water. The carcass was hung upside down from the central beam of the house and the fat portions of the thighs were carved out and the pieces of flesh heaped together. Some people picked up bones that still had some flesh sticking to them. They burnt these in the fire and dipping them in salt, enjoyed every bone.

Finally the big pot with the mutton was on the fire. The pungent smell of masala made many mouths water. They all flocked around the curry-pot, for it was more than six months since mutton had been cooked in that village.

Then they made their way to the dry village pond and offered pinda to please the dead. The old woman was ritually made into a widow: the kumkuma was put on her forehead and then wiped off. The sons and the grandsons had their heads shaved. Other close relatives got their beards and moustaches shaved.

With all the kinsfolk gathered together, the atmosphere was full of laughter and jokes. 'When my aunt pushes off I shall order two sheep,' said one; while the other declared that he would get three sheep cooked when his uncle died. 'You misers, wait and see, I am going to get four sheep killed and cooked. I intend to observe the rites for my grandfather ever so grandly,' boasted another. Joking, they took their ritual baths at the village well and returned home for the feast.

And there was such a rush.

It was ages since anyone had eaten rice and that too with mutton curry. They were so famished that they started gulping down the food, afraid even to chew, as if this might delay the second helping. But the tough mutton that hadn't softened in spite of the coconut and the green chillies, left them gasping. The sheer effort involved in eating made them sweat and sigh. Yet, the moment did come when loin threads felt tight and dhotis had to be loosened around the waist.

Parents were busy feeding the children seated by their side. Whenever a child was about to get up, satiated, his parent gave him a few thumps on the back and made him sit down and eat some more. They yelled at their stupid children, 'Bastards, you've all this fine rice and mutton curry and you say, Enough. Scoundrels! You won't eat your fill here and will start crying for more once you're home. Why can't you eat now?' The idea was to skip a meal or two after the feast.

Then the Brahmin was called to sprinkle holy water.

He was given rice, lentils, jaggery, black sesame seeds and a brand new stainless steel chembu. The Brahmin reeled off the mantras, punctuating the recitation by asking for various daanas of gold, new clothes, cows and innumerable other items — gifts from those who had no proper cloth to cover their bodies! In place of the actual gifts the priest magnanimously offered auspicious rice grains as substitutes and so the ceremony came to an end. Finally he asked for his dakshina. This time the real thing; subsitutes wouldn't do.

A drunken relative pleaded, 'Swami, my uncle desired to eat mutton in his last days but died without eating any. His spirit is sure to be hovering right here tormented by the unfulfilled desire. Please chant the mantras with enough vigour to send his soul into the upper regions.'

Mareppa placed a ten-rupee note in the Brahmin's palm.

The Brahmin looked at the money, looked up at the sky and again at the money and said, 'The soul of the departed is still in the middle region and the amount offered is not enough to make him ascend.' He added with a laugh, 'The man died with an unfulfilled desire, you should add at least another five rupees.'

'Yes that's right, give five more — when the Swami recites his mantras and sprinkles the holy water all the inauspiciousness is bound to disappear,' advised the drunken relative.

A hapless Mareppa reluctantly placed another five rupees on the floor.

The Brahmin dipped mango leaves into the holy water and sprinkled it on all present. The whole lot — adults and children — were eager to get a few drops on their heads. A few paid ten paise and five paise and had an extra sprinkling performed on the heads of their children.

The Brahmin collected all the money rice and other items besides his bus fare. He left with a smile.

Satisfied with a full meal, the guests slowly started leaving.

On the third day after this event, the widow started crying.

'You old fool,' her sons rebuked her, 'why do you cry for someone who is dead and gone. The Lord called him and he went. How long will a ripe fruit stay on the branch?'

'You!' spat the old woman. 'You spent three hundred rupees to buy a sheep and then cooked it with masala. All the bitches and bastards in the village vied with each other to have their fill. They ate till their gorge rose. And you demons never thought of throwing me even a few bones . . . . You animals ate all the bones and poured the watery gravy into my plate. May the gods curse you. May your leaf-plates be torn to shreds. May the wombs of your womenfolk be barren forever. May your tribe cease to prosper . . .'

THE FULL MOON IN WINTER

DILIP PURUSHOTTAM CHITRE

nominated by Vilas Sarang
translated by Suhas Gole

I saw Antya approaching in that special rolling walk of his. He was wearing his lawyer's black jacket and had with him his brief-case laden with papers. He broke into a broad smile when he saw me and waved his hand in greeting. We met outside the Bombay High Court and getting out onto the University side, we crossed Mahatma Gandhi Road and went down the opposite street to our usual bar. We ordered two quarter bottles of gin before either of us said a word.

It was noon and very hot. Having gin wasn't such a good idea really but it was an old habit of ours — to drink when we met. Thirty years back when we were in college together the State of

The Full Moon in Winter (title of the original story) was first published in Marathi in *Gulmohar* Diwali issue, 1989.

Maharashtra had not yet come into existence. Mr. Morarjee Desai, the Chief Minister of Bombay, was determined to impose prohibition. We drank country liquor on the sly. Our entire group met at clandestine hooch joints in various parts of the city. We are past fifty now. There are distilleries all over Maharashtra and not only is there no prohibition but drinking has become a socially acceptable vice. Those of us who had once broken the law to drink country liquor of the first-distillate variety were the brave pioneers. No way we can give up an old habit.

Antya is the oldest friend to have stayed in touch. He's a lawyer and I am a writer. I have taken up various occupations to earn my living while I carried on with my writing. Antya invariably helped me out when I was in difficulties. I've not been able to stick to either a house or a job for any length of time, while Antya has lived and worked on steadily. We've managed our families each in our own way. Antya and I have continued to meet, and when we do, we drink and we talk not only about ourselves but about everything under the sun. No other friendship gives me as much. Since our college days we have spent time like this, watching the happenings in the world and making learned comments on them. It is our way of savouring the world. All these years of discussion have made us realise how different we are from each other and yet how similar. The liquor is only a pretext.

I was uneasy today. Every friendship has its own unwritten codes: I do not tell Antya when I am in difficulty. There are many things about my life that he knows nothing about. He might, at best, be able to imagine them. I have lived not only in various parts of India, but in Europe, America and Africa. And I have moved about in spheres as diverse as clerkdom, government service, journalism, teaching, advertising, cinema and art. I am intense by nature and I have been involved with more women than most. This has been the cause of great complications and tensions in my personal life but I have resolved them in my own way. Antya may or may not have known this, but until I've raised the issues, he has never said anything on his own in this or any other matter. He will not badger me with questions — it is not his way. He won't even think I am being secretive.

'Do you remember Lalita Honavar, Antya?'

'You mean the one from college — *The Full Moon in Winter?*'

'Yes, that's the one.'

'Whatever made you remember her after all these years?'

'I'll tell you. But first tell me what you remember about her. You have a wonderful memory.'

'Well, her father was an ICS officer. Quite the Englishman. Got involved in some scandal or the other and committed suicide.'

'What about the girl?'

'Great looking but so cold that no one ever thought of making a pass at her. That's what earned her the title The Full Moon in Winter. Snobbish. Only spoke English. Never mixed with anyone. And her subject — Sociology! She was either a year senior or junior to us — she wasn't in our class in the first year.'

'What else?'

'Nothing more. This is the first time her name has cropped up after all these years. What's up?'

'Nothing. I've had a phone call from her.'

'Oh?'

'Yes.'

'What about?'

'She's the President of some women's organisation. She's invited me to give a talk. She said on the phone that she had a feeling we had gone to the same college and asked me if I remembered her name. And like a fool I said, Yes, of course.'

'You shouldn't have done that. Why, the bitch never so much as looked at anybody. Thought she was the best. You should have done the same thing now. Well, what then?'

'I met her. She's as old as us — over fifty — but looks every bit as she did at college. Probably dyes her hair. Hasn't married. Still a Miss.'

'What use is that to us so late in our lives? You are a grandfather and my children are adolescents.'

'I'm just informing you.'

'What's the point?'

'She wanted to know if I've kept in touch with anybody from college. So I told her about you. She was very surprised to hear that we still meet regularly; and she was curious to know what we did when we met, what we talked about. I told her that we sit and drink, listen to old records, talk about old times and practically everything else.'

'Then?'

'She said, How fantastic! I would love to join you one evening if I am invited. Just to observe two friends talk. I've never experienced such a thing myself! I was a bit taken aback. I said, Yes, of course, but I think you'll be disappointed. There's nothing in it really. But she insisted and I told her I would let her know after I had spoken to you.'

'My dear chap, how's that possible? Are our meetings stage shows to be commissioned by whoever wants them?'

'But she's rung up thrice after that.'

'So?'

'Are you free this Saturday?'

'What? Oh, well, yes.'

'I have called her to my place. Said I'd confirm it after I spoke to you.'

'God! But it's all right — she'll get bored and leave on her own.'

'It'll be the usual thing. As you know there's no one at home now. We'll have a cold buffet: I'll get it from somewhere. It's settled then?'

'If you say so. But to tell you the truth, I still can't believe it.'

That settled, we drank gin to our heart's content and having talked as usual, went back home.

I was to be alone in the house all of next week. My wife, son, daughter-in-law and grandson are in Pune. That's where we mainly live these days. When I come to Bombay on work I stay in a friend's flat; he has gone abroad and has left the keys with me. The flat has all the amenities including a phone. It's centrally situated — at Worli — an affluent locality, and peaceful, so I can concentrate on my work. As I grow older, I too have begun to look for all the maximum comfort and convenience I can get. The hectic pace that once used to add to my excitement has become hateful. Besides, there's this ischaemia hanging like a sword over my head.

I do not go out much. I cook my own food. But I love cooking; trying out new dishes gives me great pleasure. For the last few days I have been busy doing some preliminary work on a film. I am preparing a detailed shooting script from a screenplay I'd written earlier. The location for the shooting, the cast and even the dates have been decided on. It remains now to decide on the tenor of each scene and divide the shots on that basis — the angle for each shot, the distance between the camera and the subject, the lighting, whether to keep the camera still or moving, the direction and speed at which the camera is to move, the movement of the characters and their gestures and actions, the highs and lows of the dialogue and the timbre of the voices, the props and things needed for the scenes, the costumes and their colour, the other sounds to be recorded apart from the dialogue, the background music, and the points at which it starts and ends, the order of the prints for editing and their stacking. I try and put down as many minute details as possible. Many of these will be altered at the last moment but I believe that if the whole team can have a clear picture of what the film is finally going to be like, each one can put his heart into the work and give his best.

I had invited Lalita Honavar for Saturday evening but I began to hate myself for it. Antya was coming and she was coming, which meant that the whole of Saturday would be spent getting things ready and in taking care of the guests. Drinks and a late night would mean that all of Sunday morning would be spent lazing around. That would be two whole days gone. But it was too late to cancel the programme now.

Putting together a cold meal is even more difficult than making a hot one. A hot meal goes down even if it is not very tasty but preparing a meal to go with drinks is more difficult. I had to get butter, mustard and mayonnaise for the sandwiches, boiled eggs and boneless chicken, ham and steamed pomfret with the bones removed, onion cut to order, tomatoes, pink radish, mint and garlic chutney, boiled chana and minced corriander leaves, besides farsan, roasted peanuts and chana, slices of cheese, apple, cashew nuts, two bottles of gin, a dozen bottles of soda, fresh lime juice and lime cordial, angostura bitters, orange and pineapple juice, chilled beer in case anyone wanted it, and Riesling wine. I'd barely finished organising all this and had put on my silk kurta after a bath when Antya arrived.

'What! All this for that cold woman? Looks like a feast! Haven't we always managed on just gin and chana?'

'Enjoy yourself Antya, enjoy yourself. I've been given an advance for the film.'

'That's interesting. You've actually received your payment on time, have you?'

'How am I to know whether I'll get the rest of the instalments? But the producer was in a great hurry.'

'Fine. Now tell me, when is this female coming?'

'Seven-thirty. There's still an hour left. Do you want to change? Have a wash?'

'Okay. I want to take off my coat and tie. By the way, how much do you pay for this flat?'

'Why should I pay? This is Bharat's flat and he's gone to America.'

'Who's this Bharat?'

'Bharat Patel. He's originally from Uganda—he came here during the Idi Amin days. We got acquainted, and the acquaintance grew.'

'Why don't you put on some music? Do you have anything classical?'

'Vocal or instrumental?'

'Vocal. Put on a concert tape. Do you have anything by Panditji?' Panditji is Krishnarao Shankar Pandit; we have been his admirers since we were children.

It's a first class concert. 1965 vintage. Starts with a *khayal*, a *chees* and a *tarana* in the raag Yaman. Then the Nand raag. Followed by a *tappa* in Kafi. Then Shankara. Then a *thumri* in Tilang, followed by a *chatrang* in Malkauns. After that Basant, Jogiya and Lalit, right up to the finale in Bhairavi.

'It must have been a four-hour session!'

'And all sung with such vigour. Absolutely fullbodied.'

I put on the tape and almost absentmindedly, we started drinking.

The doorbell rang. I opened the door and there was Lalita Honavar.

'Come in!'

'Sorry, I'm late.'

She was wearing a purple silk sari with a green and turmeric-yellow border. Her hair was tied up in a tight knot and she was wearing typical Maharashtrian eartops. Her fair, yellowish complexion was set off by the sari. She entered, bringing in with her a whiff of expensive French perfume. I introduced Antya.

'I have seen him in college.'

Antya is an outspoken person. 'How could you have seen the likes of us,' he said, 'you never cared so much as to look at anyone. Besides, during the four years of college we rarely went to classes.'

'Your crowd sat on the steps of the Liberty Laundry every morning. Once one of you had said something and all of you had a good laugh at my expense.'

'That wasn't me. It was a chap called Oak.'

'That forward chap with a flat nose and light eyes?'

'Exactly. You have a good memory.'

'Anyone would have noticed your lot! You were in the college, yet went about as if you weren't. Of course, you weren't any trouble to anybody but you were universally known for the way you ogled at every girl and gave everyone — students and professors — the most peculiar nicknames.'

'What will you drink?' I asked. 'We're having gin but if gin doesn't suit you, there's Riesling wine or beer or fruit juice.'

'I'd like some wine.'

I gave her some.

'Cheers!'

'Well, carry on. I am an unwanted guest really. I couldn't help being curious about two college friends who keep meeting regularly even after they are past fifty. You probably know that I'm a student of Sociology. I have written a book on the loneliness of women. I propose to write a similar book on men.'

'We agree that we are men,' said Antya, 'and we also agree that we cannot live without drinks. But how do you gather we are lonely?'

'He is a lawyer by profession,' I said, 'you must be careful.'

'No wonder he began cross-examining me as if I had made an accusation. Now look, I haven't come here to study you. When I heard that the two of you have met regularly for the last thirty to thirty-five years and still spend hours talking to each other, I was amazed. This man's a writer, you are a lawyer; you are so different in nature and by profession. And yet . . . .'

'You are making yet another assumption. My dear lady, even if Antya is a lawyer today there was a time when he wrote poetry. We are both equally fond of songs and films, besides enjoying each other's company. We used to take bhang and smoke charas and ganja and wander all over the city. Now we only drink liquor. We have seen to it that our habits never cause anyone any trouble. What we really like is to listen to music and talk to each other when we are drunk.'

No one said anything for some time. The tape was still playing. The Nand raag got over and the tappa in Kafi began, *Miya Janewale*, the most loved of the tappas that flash like swords in the arsenal of the Gwalior gharana. All the great exponents, from Krishnarao Shankar Pandit and Rajabhaiya Poonchwale, right up to Sharatchandra Arolkar and Jal Balaporia have sung it. The composition remains the same but every singer weaves into it his own colours. It has all the subtle tenderness of a maiden's plea to a lover leaving for distant lands. Panditji is basically a very masculine singer. His bass, sinewy and full of mingled notes like music played on the been, is his speciality. But when he sings this tappa . . . the amazing range and wonderful abandon, the scintillating highlights, the cascades of mingled swaras, the persuasive returns to the dominant notes, the overpowering artistry makes you want to listen to it over and over again.

'*Allah . . . di kasama . . . twanoo . . . .*'

Antya had forgotten that Lalita Honavar existed. He had closed his eyes and was beating time and bursting into exclamations of delight whenever Panditji, making detours and feints, returned with a delicate modulation to the major beat.

'Who is the singer?' Lalita asked me in a low voice.

'Krishnarao Shankar Pandit of Gwalior. This classical stuff isn't boring you, I hope?'

'Oh no! It's not that. In fact, one of my sisters is a singer. But I do not understand Indian classical music; it sounds unfamiliar. I have listened more often to Western music. All my education was in English. We speak Konkani at home. I know Marathi because I've lived in Bombay, but I don't speak it fluently. My father was an ICS officer. . . and he only spoke to us in English.'

The tappa ended.

'Stop the tape for some time,' said Antya, 'it will be difficult to take it all in at one go.'

I stopped the tape.

Being the host, I had to serve the drinks and pass the snacks around. Lalita's behaviour really astonished me. She had already consumed three quarters of the wine in the bottle, and she wasn't neglecting the food either. She was watching us closely, particularly Antya.

Antya however, was lost in his own world. At one point he brought up the subject of Madan Mohan, the music director, and I started telling them how Madan Mohan had used the single raag Bageshree for the composition of a number of very difficult tunes. I even sang out the sections. After that we talked about some other friends. It turned out that someone we knew at college had become a big-time smuggler. Then we talked about someone else whose wife had come to Antya with her divorce case and how Antya had given her brief to another lawyer.

The chunk of society that we make up produces clerks, salesmen, doctors, engineers and lawyers. Some are poor or have become poor, some are rich, but most belong to the middle class. Some have gone abroad; others have scattered to various parts of the country; but most have remained in Bombay. Some have become famous cricketers; some have joined politics; some have become contractors or businessmen and some have even joined the theatre and cinema. Antya has all the latest information on everyone. Whenever and wherever he meets any of them, he invariably inquires after them. He carries in his head a prodigious file of information about his contemporaries. I am sure the latest information on Lalita Honavar had already gone into that file. If someone wanted to write a composite history of Ruia College, Antya could have easily written about the 1950s and 60s without a break. Even after he had received his degree, he and a few other friends continued to frequent the college for some years. Besides, some of our friends had become professors. Even as he quietly practised his own profession, Antya kept a close tag on the history of his own times.

I noticed that Lalita Honavar had become absolutely still as she listened to him.

'If you don't mind, will you give me a perfectly clear answer to a question I am about to ask you? Both of you.'

'We've had so much to drink,' said Antya, 'that even a perfectly clear answer might not seem clear enough.'

'Ask,' I said.

'What exactly does The Full Moon in Winter mean?'

'Well, in Marathi we used to say the pournima in winter.'

'I am not asking you for that kind of an explanation. Why did you give a particular person that name? What did it mean when it was applied to me?'

'I shall try and explain,' I said, 'but after all these years, you mustn't read anything personal into it. Remember that we are speaking of boys who thirty-five years ago were on the threshold of youth and who could not, very easily, have the company of young girls. Agreed?'

'Agreed. Go on.'

'You were fair and goodlooking. You belonged to the upper caste and the upper crust. We came from Marathi-medium schools and from the lower middle class. You spoke very good English . . . you moved about with an air of self-importance . . . you had a starched look . . . behaved as if the rest of the world were inferior and of no consequence. We never saw you speak or smile freely with anyone. You kept a certain distance. . . so, it was The Full Moon. And because you were beautiful and since you remained aloof and were difficult to understand, In Winter. What do you say, Antya?'

'Put it as you will. You are the poet.'

'But you are a lawyer and this conversation is like a courtroom exchange. I think that this is really an accusation.'

'She hasn't yet made a complaint.'

'But tell me, did it never occur to you that the title you bestowed on her would have an effect on her mind?'

'Now look, we waited for four years for it to have an effect. You never even turned around to look. There were plenty of girls who would hit back, threaten us with their chappals, complain to the Principal. Their reaction was an acknowledgement of sorts, it showed that they had noticed us. Some of them even began to talk freely with us after that.'

'Not a single girl ever spoke to me during the four years I was at college,' said Antya. 'Once to make fun of me, one of the girls from a group came up to me and innocently asked if a particular road went to Matunga station. I said Yes, and the girls began laughing.'

'How silly!'

'But at that age the silliness had quite a different meaning. They had found me alone and looking absentminded and must have decided to make a fool of me. It was their way of avenging the honour of the group, because usually every girl who passed by was sure to be rewarded with a verbal present.'

'Shall I return to the subject? What if the label you attached to me, proclaiming me as an insensitive, unfeeling, hypocritical, vain, misanthropic girl, had an adverse effect? You are a lawyer, aren't you? Well, tell me, was this not defaming me? And what if this sobriquet you gave me inflicted a deep injury on my mind and ruined my future?'

'Miss Honavar, if I were stating your case as your lawyer, I would have to prove that you were defamed. I would also have to produce evidence of the harm done to your psyche. Perhaps the American law would have been more useful to you than ours.'

'If you are a lawyer, you can also be a judge. Don't you think injustice has been done to me?'

'My God! Miss Honavar!'

'I am perfectly serious,' Lalita Honavar said, extending her empty wine glass for a refill.

I filled it up and returned it to her. Antya said, 'Excuse me,' and went into the bathroom.

'I hope you aren't upset.'

'I'm all right. I really shouldn't have brought this up. Our lawyer friend seems to be a trifle upset.'

Antya, who was on his way back from the bathroom, overheard this last remark and like a character making his entry on the stage, said on cue, 'My mind does not normally get upset. But my stomach sometimes does. Do we have a plain soda?'

I opened a bottle of soda for him.

'If an act of verbal aggression or indiscretion has been committed unknowingly, one can apologise and expect to receive a token punishment. Newspaper editors very often get away by tendering an apology.'

'But is teasing a girl so different from a defamation in a newspaper? When editors make mistakes, it is considered to be an occupational hazard; after all one prints opinions or news for the common good of the people. Their intentions are never doubted. But passing remarks about a girl whom one does not even know is like slinging mud at random. There's no question of the common good in this sort of practice shooting.'

'You're right in principle. But, in practice, such light-hearted teasing is part of the fun in school and college life. It is not good to ban fun.'

'You will soon call ragging fun and rape fun.'

'Certainly not. But do you have any objections to calling a joke a joke?'

'It all depends on what makes you laugh. Idi Amin used to find the atrocities he perpetrated on his prisoners very funny.'

'What are you trying to say? Is calling you The Full Moon in Winter a moral offense, a heinous crime?'

'First let me ask *him* a question. He is a poet. What do the words suggest?'

'The Full Moon in Winter is like an image in a typical Chinese or Japanese poem. It can imply a number of things.'

'In the context of a woman?'

'The full moon or pournima could be a figurative description of a beautiful face.'

'And winter?'

'That would depend on the context.'

'If the context isn't given, it would make the metaphor suggestive and mysterious.'

'One must also consider the country,' said Antya. 'The winter of Siberia is different from the winter of our Karnataka.'

'If the meaning is basically ambiguous it cannot be said that it is only defamatory.'

So far Lalita Honavar had been speaking in a quiet restrained tone. Now suddenly she lost her poise. She was like an angry spitting cat as she said, 'This is what I call male doubletalk. You can only think of woman as a plaything whether in poetry or in real life! When you called me The Full Moon in Winter, you implied that I was cold-blooded and frigid, a frozen girl. Some of you even called me Miss Iceberg. You were really taking revenge on me for ignoring your covetous male eyes. You ought to realise this at least now that you are past fifty. If I'd met your eyes with mine, replied to your questions, gone around with one of you, I would have been acceptable. You wanted to drag me into your fold at any cost.'

The room had become very still. Her venemous outburst had made us tense. When she rose and went to the bathroom, Antya said to me in a low voice, 'Hell! It's getting complicated. Beware of the woman. I'm off.'

'No you're not. Please stay on. I can't handle this alone.'

Miss Honavar returned from the bathroom and said, 'I'm really enjoying this. I'm a stranger among you and yet I feel so free. It's as though we were friends at college.'

'We didn't have a single girlfriend in college. I've never had one since. He may have — he's travelled all over the world. As for me, I am a simple man. I got married, brought my wife home and settled down right away.'

'You didn't have any girlfriends in college?'

'Well, I wasn't swanky and I wasn't rich; I had lofty aims but I wasn't clever; nor was I a sportsman or an actor or a singer. It is not enough in our country to be just a man to be able to have girlfriends.'

'I've read novels by that Nemade of yours. He speaks of a category of bachelor men — kare lok.'

'What do you think, is she right?' Antya asked me.

'I haven't read much of Nemade. I only remember his *Kosla*.'

'But what about you?' Miss Honavar said, turning to me. 'They say women are central to your writings. But I think you make a woman either an animal or a goddess.'

'You are dragging me to court, aren't you?'

'Your best friend is a laywer.'

'My friend is unlikely to have read everything I've written. That is why we are friends. He'll defend me if it is anything else. But he will find it difficult to defend my writings. In other words I am defenceless.'

'Shall I ask you a question?' said Miss Honavar. 'But before that, give me a stiff drink.'

I saw Antya grow serious. He looked worried. Nevertheless, I mustered up enough courage to ask, 'Will gin do? There isn't much of a choice. Or would you rather have rum? Or brandy?'

'Brandy? I'd love some. Ple — ease.'

Ple — ease? That was the limit. I poured out brandy for her in a fresh glass.

'Thanks.' She took a small gulp. I gulped down all my gin.

'Ask your question.'

'It is a delicate one.'

'What can be more delicate than what we have already discussed?'

You are both married . . . You have children, I presume.'

'I have a son. He has a son and a daughter.'

'The children have come of age?'

'Well, yes. My son's married. I have a grandson who is four years old.'

'Your wives have lived happily with you for several years?'

'This our wives alone can say,' said Antya.

'Some thirty to thirty-five years ago you teased and bestowed on me the title The Full Moon in Winter. But suppose I had at that time responded to one of you and then, as in Hindi films, the acquaintance had grown into a close friendship, would you have married me?'

'That would have been impossible in my case,' said Antya, 'because I am originally from Karnataka. After all my years in Bombay I speak Marathi like a Maharashtrian, but my English has never been good and I could never have coped with a wife who came from an English-medium school.'

'Why?'

'Well, I haven't been able to answer back my wife either in Kannada or Marathi. It would be out of the question in English!'

'And what do *you* say?'

'It is a tantalising question, Miss Honavar,' I said. 'My English isn't bad. And at that time — I may say that even now you are very, very attractive.'

'In the long run no wife is attractive.'

'I still find my wife attractive.'

'Sare Jahan se achchha Hindustan hamara!'

When he heard this Antya burst out laughing. He too began to sing. *'Hum bulbule hai iske, ye gulistan hamara . . . .*

'You are very sexy, Miss Honavar,' I said, 'I don't think I could resist you!'

'That's all right in theory. But I am past my childbearing age and yet, not only am I unmarried, I am also a virgin.'

The bell rang at this point. I opened the door.

'Hi, Dipi! Oh, Antya! What's on? Are you having a party?'

It was Damu. He was wearing a tie and carrying a bag full of medical samples. Then he saw Lalita Honavar and stopped short.

'Miss Honavar, meet my friend, Damu. He is not a college friend; we met later. Damu, this is Miss Honavar. She was with us at college.'

'Hullo!'

'What will you drink, Damu? And what would you like to eat? Everything's on the table.'

'Don't bother yourselves. I'll just go in for a wash.'

And Damu made straight for the bathroom.

'This is Damu. He's a pharmaceutical salesman, playwright,

short story writer, poet and lover of life.'

'He's turned up so unexpectedly and so late?'

'All my friends come like that. Punctuality is for business matters.'

'It's getting to be a crowd!'

'Damu's a fantastic man.'

'And past fifty?'

'All fantastic men are past fifty, Miss Honavar. But what difference does that make?'

Damu returned. 'Sorry friends, sorry Miss Honavar. Sorry for the interruption.'

'Thank you for the interruption,' said Antya. 'It was desperately needed.'

'Shall we go to the balcony?' Lalita Honavar asked.

We went to the balcony which overlooked the sea. A salty breeze blew in.

'On second thoughts,' I said, 'I too think I wouldn't have married you.'

'Oh, how disappointing! But why?'

'I can't see even now how I could have controlled you.'

'Does marriage mean having control over one another?'

'Yes, it is mutual control — a sensible rivalry to authority.'

'And I'm not sensible?'

'Sensible people don't remain virgin till they are fifty.'

'Why?'

'Virginity is related to the body. The body must age and with age there are changes in what the body means. After menopause a woman is no longer a woman. She doesn't become a man of course, but she becomes just a person.'

'And this *person* has no sex life?'

'Of course, she has. Human beings never cease to have a sex life. But towards the end it gradually becomes meaningless.'

'Meaningless? Is being able to give birth to children the only meaning you attach to a sex life?'

'As I see it, sex can mean two things: One is orgasm or sexual gratification; the other is procreation. The first represents a desire to break free from nature; the second is an assimilation into it. When it is not possible for you to have a child or when you don't want one, it means you want to be free from nature, be free of any obligation to human society. In the Indian tradition, sex for the sole purpose of self-gratification is regarded as asocial. The sexual union of Shiva and Shakti was responsible for the creation of human society, but Shiva and Shakti still remain absorbed in each other. Their separation will bring the deluge. The end of creation. The regeneration of man depends on the union of the two sexes. If a man and woman do not come together, the cycle of existence will stop as far as man is concerned. But even before we acquire the ability to reproduce, we have, even at a very young age, the rudiments of sexual desire. Even when the reproductive capability comes to an end in old age, the marks of sexuality remain. Sexuality is inseparably linked with living. When a woman is past her reproductive age, the age of procreation, she does not lose her sexuality. Have you seen autumn in the colder countries? The leaves take on such vivid colours before they fall. And when they have fallen, the leafless trees continue to stand through the cold snowy winter. They do not die. In the spring they bring out new leaves.'

'And you had called me The Full Moon in Winter,' she said, 'the pournima in winter, a moon shining on a barren landscape when life is ended.'

'Sorry, Miss Honavar. But there is really no relation between that remark we made in our youth and what I have just said. Please do not allow the misunderstanding to grow.'

'I have not misunderstood anything,' said Miss Honavar.

Miss Honavar was seated in the armchair with her eyes closed. Antya had put on Panditji's tape again. He was singing a piece from the Basant raag: *Piya sang khelori*.

'Who is this woman, Dipi?' Damu asked in a confidential

undertone, 'She's a real peach! Haven't you laid her yet? I think she is up to something! It's just as in a story. Antya told me she was with you at college and that you didn't even know her then. And now she has suddenly turned up on some pretext and has stuck to you. Have fun, Dipi. Shall I take Antya away?'

'Why don't you and Antya escort her home instead? She has her car.'

'In that case she can drop us where we can find a taxi.'

There was a movement in the armchair. Miss Honavar emptied her glass and looking in our direction said, 'Are you conspiring to get rid of me? I don't feel like going home. This is the first time I've been alone in the company of three men.'

'Relax!' Damu said. 'It's my first experience too, drinking with a single woman in the company of two men.'

'Tell me,' she said, 'why do you men always get together to have drinks?'

'Brotherhood,' Damu said. 'Solidarity.'

Antya woke up. 'Shall I tell you?' he asked, 'there are many things that are not to be said in front of women.'

'We talk about women among ourselves,' Damu said. 'That's not something women can understand. Because women never understand what they are from a man's point of view.'

'Are you woman-haters?'

'Not at all. As a matter of fact I love women.'

'Love them or make love to them?' I asked.

'No. I am a bhokto as they say in Bengali, a devotee.'

'You are a parambhakta,' I said, 'a super devotee.'

'This party is turning into a fantasy.'

'I've heard and also read that when there is a lone woman with several men, she is likely to be gang-raped.'

There was a glint in Damu's eyes. 'Is that your fantasy?'

'Who said that only the body can be raped?' said Miss Honavar. 'The mind can also be raped. When we were in college, these people used to call me The Full Moon in Winter. The whole college came to know of it. They used to call me Miss Iceberg!'

'I would have called you Miss Icefruit. You are so juicy.'

'Careful, Damu!' I muttered.

'But I don't find you cold at all,' said Damu. 'You look so lovely, so warm. These chaps did not really understand.'

'You are flattering me.'

'I am complimenting you because I can't help it,' said Damu, going towards her. Antya looked very apprehensive. His straightforward, innocent mind could not approve of what was happening.

'You are pulling my leg!'

'I am being pulled into orbit around you,' said Damu. And he actually spun round like a medieval knight in an English film and went down on one knee to kiss her hand. But when she started laughing hysterically he was completely bewildered.

'There's something of medieval chivalry still left then,' said Miss Honavar.

'Damu was born in the fourteenth century,' I said.

'I'm from the twenty-second century,' she said. 'I see little difference between the fourteenth and the twentieth century. There used to be men, they say, in those times.'

'You mean there won't be any men at all in the twenty-second century?' Antya asked.

'But our remnants will certainly last,' said Damu. 'Why are you all so concerned about history? Good men are born at all times. Excuse me, I'd like to change into a lungi. I want to sit on the floor.' And he picked up his black bag and went inside. When he returned he was wearing a bright red lungi and was carrying a snake-charmer's pipe.

'What's this,' I said spotting the snake-charmer's pipe in his hand.

'It's a new retailing aid our company has given us; there is a snake in the bag,' he announced and opened the bag.

As soon as he started playing the pipe, a snake came out.

Miss Honavar shrieked and ran to me. Holding me in a frightened embrace, she shouted, 'Please, ple-ase, put that creature back in the bag.'

'This cobra has had its poison removed,' said Damu. 'He's just an earthworm in disguise. He only *looks* like a snake!'

'Where did you learn to play that thing, Damu?'

'A multinational company trains you well. We were taken to Khajuraho for our course, and we were put up at the Chandela Hotel for eight days. There were lectures and discussions in the morning, followed by lunch, and then we had the pipe-playing sessions. After that, video shows, then drinks and finally, dinner. Occasionally, we had time-off to go look at the erotic sculptures in the temples. It was fun. I put on eight kilos in a week.'

And he began to play his pipe again.

'Take that horrible creature away!' Miss Honavar cried out again and again. 'Take it away or I shall faint.'

Miss Honavar had now been shifted to my bedroom.

Bharat Patel who owned the place, had on the wall a print of Velazquez's *The Toilette of Venus*. A nude Venus is lying asleep on her side, her back to the viewers. She is looking at herself in the mirror. Of course, that was the only way one could have seen her face.

Lalita Honavar was also lying on her side. Though her sari was somewhat disarranged, she was certainly not nude. According to Damu, the drinks had gone to her head.

Antya, however, was of the opinion that I should call a doctor. We hardly knew her and she was over fifty; if anything happened to her, we'd find it difficult explaining the circumstances. Antya must have thought of this as a lawyer, but it was also what common-sense pointed to.

'Whose painting is this?'

'Diego Velazquez. A famous seventeenth-century painter.'

'Who's the woman?'

'Venus.'

'What is it called?'

'*The Toilette of Venus.*'

'*The Full Moon in Winter*,' Miss Honavar mumbled. 'The name of that painting is *The Full Moon in Winter*. Who's hung it there?'

'How are you feeling, Miss Honavar?'

'Fine! Fine! Never felt bet' in m' life, darling. Can I have some more wine?'

She sat up suddenly and looking at me with heavy eyes, said: 'So you did bring me into your bedroom finally, didn't you? And there are three of you. There was only this bedroom scene left.'

'You had too much drink. You passed out.'

'That's what you think. I think I've not had enough. It was the snake that made me faint. Where's that snake gone?'

'He must have got to our head-office at Worli. He slipped out of here in the confusion.'

'What use is your pipe now?'

'The pipe, too, belongs to the Company. We use it instead of the medical samples nowadays.'

'You are a tricky bastard,' she said. 'But I like you! Get me some wine. Let's all have another drink. Come, get the glasses, the glasses! This bed's very comfortable — we can all fit in quite easily!'

'You mean we should all sleep here?' Damu asked, feeling very happy at the thought.

'The joint-family system is out,' said Antya.

'Long ago, we little boys and girls used to sleep like that in a line. That's why we had no need for sex education later.'

'We are all past fifty,' Miss Honavar said. 'Sexually speaking, a very different chapter in our life has begun.'

'This is called a second adolescence. It is followed by a second childhood and then, a second infancy.'

'And finally, rebirth!'

'Here's the wine! Where did these bottles come from?'

'They were kept in reserve. I had left them to be chilled. And here are some nuts.'

Damu began to sing:

Give me no 'buts'
Have cashew nuts -
O Love, youth goes by . . .

'Where did you get that song from?'

'It's a pada from my new play.'

'A shwapada or animal rather, considering it's four-footed.'

'What's the new play called?'

'*Alibaag and the Forty Thieves.*'

'Alibaag?'

'Yes, Alibaag. That's a great place. You get good fish there, and the coastline is beautiful.'

'But they say the builders from Bombay have spoilt it now.'

'It's a great place I say. Witchcraft everywhere. I met a mantrik there. If you have an enemy, let me know. I'll arrange to give him hydrocele.'

'Why hydrocele of all things?'

'He must be fond of playing marbles,' said Antya.

'He gave me a couple of enchanted eggs once, this mantrik. Said I should make an omelette of them and give it to the woman I wished to seduce. I brought them home and they broke, and the cat in our building ate them. Now the cat always comes only to our house.'

'And if the cat were to have kittens, you would say you are the natural father . . . .'

'Miss Honavar, do you believe in witchcraft?'

'I didn't. But from now on I'm not going to eat an omelette prepared by someone I don't know.'

'My dear chap,' Antya said, 'it's almost morning. It's two-thirty. I'll sleep outside on the settee, or do you have another bedroom?'

'There's one on the other side.'

'Then I'm going there. I can't handle late nights any more. Goodnight!'

'Goodnight, Mr. Lawyer.'

When Antya had gone, Lalita Honavar pulled her legs up on to the bed to sit more comfortably. She took a gulp of wine, looked at Damu, took another gulp, looked at me, then stretched herself.

'Sorry to bother you,' she said, 'but can you give me something to wear for the night? I think your size will do. A kurta, perhaps? I can do without pajamas.'

I opened the cupboard that faced us. There were two muslin kurtas and one silk kurta inside — three in all. I placed them before her and said, 'Take your pick.' She chose a muslin one.

'Come, Dipu, we'll sit outside,' said Damu.

Damu and I went and sat outside in the living-room.

'Dipu!' Damu whispered. 'Go in and enjoy yourself. She has been signalling for some time now. I'll sleep here outside.'

The telephone rang.

'Hello. Dilip Chitre here.'

'Hello, is Lalita Honavar there?'

It was a woman's voice.

'Hello. Who are you?'

'Geeta Honavar.'

'Please hold on.'

I was about to go in to call Lalita when she came out herself, with nothing on except the muslin kurta. I was dumbfounded. I wouldn't have been as shocked if she had been completely naked.

'Phone . . . There's a phone-call for you . . .

'Who's it?'

'Geeta.'

'Geeta? My God! Phoned here? How did she find out?'

'What shall I tell her? Or will you speak?'

'Tell her to mind her own business. She's always tailing me. Tell her she's made a mistake, that there's no Lalita Honavar here.'

I picked up the receiver again.

'Hello.'

'She won't take the phone. But let me warn you. She'll get you into trouble. Be careful. Get rid of her before it's too late.' Click.

'What did she say?'

'Nothing. She put the receiver down when she heard my voice again.'

'Bitch.'

'Who was it?'

'Geeta. Geeta Honavar. My sister and my arch enemy!'

'I think she is worried about you.'

'Worried! She's always watching me. This is the sister who I said sang classical songs and was culturally very Indian. I seem to be more Western, don't I? That's my father's influence. Geeta's taken after my mother.'

'What does she do?'

'She is unmarried like me. There's no lack of money, so we don't have to worry about doing something for a living. Geeta sings occasionally on the radio or at public concerts. We live together. Tormenting me is her chief occupation. She's hated me since we were kids because she isn't good-looking. That's why she makes such a fuss about the superiority of Indian culture. Its either yoga or spirituality or else, burning agarbatti — a dozen different fads. Even as she solemnly holds the tanpura, she keeps a close watch on where I go and what I do.'

While Lalita spoke it was her body that I saw and was conscious of. She did not look a woman who had crossed fifty. She looked thirty or thirty-five. A complexion like the golden *kevda* flower, clear skin, big eyes, an oval face. She was not very high-breasted but tall and comely, with a flat stomach and below the waist, firm buttocks, well-proportioned thighs, well-moulded calves; only her feet were broad and large like a man's.

'Why are you looking at me like this? Haven't you ever seen a woman's body before?'

'I hadn't seen yours. You look very desirable, Miss Honavar.'

'You're not the first man to tell me that. But what's next?'

'Let's see what next,' I said in a gruff voice, as I pushed her in the direction of the bedroom.

Just then, Antya shouted from the adjoining bedroom, 'Where's the light? Switch on the light, someone. Snake! Snake!'

There was a snake on the bed in the other bedroom, its hood raised and expanded, and Antya was standing against the wall with a pillow in his hand. Lalita, Damu and I stood at the door.

'It did not bite you, did it?'

'It was about to, when I woke up.'

'This looks like Damu's snake.'

'This doesn't seem to be our Company snake,' Damu said, taking a close look. 'A snake from our Company has a mark like the figure ten on its hood. It's the new logo of the Company. This one belongs to our competitors. But this one too is without poison. So don't worry.'

'Play your pipe, Damu! Play it!'

'The pipe is useless. Snakes are deaf,' said Damu. 'Don't be afraid, Antya, this cobra belongs to an ayurvedic company.'

'Ayurvedic, allopathic, or homeopathic,' said Antya, 'a cobra is a cobra. It is best to kill it.'

'This is a female cobra, a nagin,' said Damu, closely examining the snake.

'How do you know?' Miss Honavar asked.

Pinching her cheek and pulling it playfully, Damu said, 'It's a female snake as surely as you are a woman. I have never made a mistake about sex so far. I can immediately recognize the female of any species. Even of plants.'

'What shall we do now?'

'Well, fetch my bag. I shall lock her up in it — she will make a nice gift for our marketing manager.'

As soon as I fetched Damu's bag for him, he caught hold of the snake and stuffed it into his bag.

Flinging away the pillow that he was holding against his chest, Antya said, 'What's the time like? It will be impossible to get any sleep after all this.'

'Three-thirty,' I replied. 'It's Sunday tomorrow, sleep up to eleven if you like.'

'It's going to be difficult to get any sleep, but I'll lie down at least. Sorry I disturbed all of you,' he said.

'What's the sorry for. If a female cobra had turned up in our beds, we'd have been just as frightened,' I said.

'If a female cobra had turned up in *my* bed, the night would have been most pleasurable,' Damu said. 'The female of the species is after all the female of the species!'

Shuddering, Miss Honavar said, 'How is it you don't feel repelled, don't feel frightened?'

I placed my open palms against Miss Honavar's waist and said, 'Come Miss Honavar, we really need to sleep, all of us.'

Damu actually winked at me and said, 'Good morning, Dilip! Good night, Miss Honavar!'

Finally, like Velasquez's Venus, Lalita Honavar shed all her clothes. But as Antya, snoring away in the neighbouring bedroom, has a very thorough knowledge of that part of the Indian Penal Code which deals with pornography, and though it doesn't matter if I am punished for a crime I did not commit (my friend after all being my lawyer) I am, at least for the present, refraining from describing our boisterous love-making.

This story is neither a long short story nor a novel; it is only a prelude. The characters and situations of 'The Full Moon in Winter' pass from truth to falsehood, from falsehood into philosophy, from philosophy to the art of love, from the art of love to poultry-keeping, from poultry-keeping to poetry, and manifest themselves in every field. To consider them purely imaginary would be an affront to Antya and Damu, but I am a law-abiding writer . . .

The phone rang again.

Now who could it be so early in the morning? Annoyed, I left Lalita at the door of the bedroom and went to the phone. On the other side Damu lay snoring peacefully.

'Hello?'

'I am Geeta Honavar.

'Speak.'

'What's the idea?'

'What about?'

'Don't pretend you don't know. I am talking about Lalita.'

'Madam, I think you're making a mistake. Who is Lalita? What number do you want?'

'I know your voice. I had dialled this very number sometime ago and you had answered. You went to call Lalita then and later the line was cut. I tried to ring up again but I kept getting a cross-connection.'

'What exactly do you want?'

'Lalita has lost her mental balance and needs psychiatric help. She tried to commit suicide last week. She has developed an obsession for the company of men and she gets violent all of a sudden. Her moods change unexpectedly, so please send her back. It's best if you bring her back yourself. Let's avoid complications as far as possible. I am sure you have understood the gravity of the situation. Good-bye!' Click.

Lalita was standing behind me.

'It was Geeta again, wasn't it? I'll tell you what she must have said: Lalita is not in her senses. She is obsessed with men. Attempts suicide. Am I right?'

'How did you know?'

'I know my sister only too well. She's told our uncle the same thing. He did not believe her, of course, but I've felt a revulsion for her since then. Did *you* think I was mad?'

From the darkness Damu was heard: 'Lali, Lali, my dear, you are mad, are you? What're you waiting for? He is a jolly good lay! He won't disappoint you. Have a good time. God will bring you together! Go, you have my blessings.'

'Damu?'

'Don't worry Dipi, I've followed everything. This is all Jhaveri's doing.'

'Jhaveri who?'

'The great grandson of Beelzebub.'

'And who is Beelzebub?'

'Lucifer! Satan himself, Allah give him peace.'

'But Damu, how does Jhaveri come in?'

'My dear chap, he's always watching us. He's our student, he studies us — he is trying to evolve into us!'

'Who are you talking about? I don't understand. The phone call was from my sister. How is she connected with Jhaveri?'

'You won't understand. Jhaveri is practising telepathy at the moment. But without their guru, those who are struggling to acquire extra-sensory powers get very confused. Their experiments go haywire. Only the other day, this Jhaveri had sent a woman to me.'

'Sent a woman to you?'

'It's all very complicated. Actually, Jhaveri had done an experiment to make her come to him. But the image he has of himself in his own mind is really that of us. He cannot recognize himself. And so there was a kind of telepathic cross-connection and thanks to the experiment he performed to seduce her, the woman came to me.'

'Who was the woman?'

'The daughter-in-law of a well-known goldsmith.'

'What did you do then, Damu?'

'Well, what could I do? When I saw the state she was in, I knew that instead of going to Jhaveri she had come to me. I felt pity. . . .'

'For whom? For Jhaveri or for her?'

'For Satan, for Freud, for Mahatma Gandhi — for everybody. Because of their queer influence, Jhaveri's experiments in magic are always going wrong. Going wrong, yes, but they are never wasted because the two of us are deep down in his mind.'

'But what has all this to do with Geeta Honavar?'

Damu laughed loudly. 'Well, Jhaveri must have started off an experiment to seduce Geeta Honavar. But he missed his mark, and in two instances at that. Instead of Geeta it was Lalita who came to you. The telepathy traffic has grown enormously of late and Jhaveri seems to be quite cursed to be constantly getting hooked to the wrong frequency. However that may be, his experiment has harmed no one. Lalita's meeting with you has taken place in line with a deeper law of nature, or how could I have thought of coming here so unexpectedly? I'd been invited to a late party by some Gujarati friends and frankly, I had completely forgotten about it. But Dipi, I thought you might be in trouble. Something guided me here.'

'What the hell!' I said, surprised.

'We are men who move in a wonderland,' said Damu. 'We must get used to it now. What use is realism after fifty?'

'Please!' Lalita Honavar said to me, 'Let's go back to the bedroom. At least you can tell me a nice story!'

'Go to bed, children,' said Damu.

Lying by my side, clinging to me, Lalita Honavar listened to my story. My voice had dissociated itself from the rest of me and sounded like a digital recording. I too was listening to my own story as I lay there by Lalita's side.

'It happened in the fourteenth century; a brahmin set out for Alandi on a pilgrimage to Dyaneshwar's samadhi . . . .'

Lalita began to run her finger over the hair on my chest. 'What kind of story is this?' she asked, 'I come from an English-medium school.'

Her French perfume was beginning to afflict me. My voice came to a halt.

'Gently . . . it's the first time.'

I began to fondle her body gently. She took off all her clothes. I began to satisfy the yearnings of her delicate body in various ways. While this quiet low-key lovemaking was in progress, the door-bell rang.

Reluctantly, but hurriedly, I drew on my trousers and went out without my shirt. Lalita shut the bedroom door from the inside. I switched on the light and opened the door, and was shocked.

'I'm Geeta Honavar. May I come in?'

'Uhn? Of course! Come, come in.'

Geeta Honavar had dark skin. She was short and somewhat stodgy, but her eyes were light and green in colour. She was wearing a sari of the purest white.

'Where is Lalita?'

'Lalita? She isn't here.'

'I can smell her!' She said, sniffing hard. 'Fragrance of *Opium* — that French perfume. It can only be her!'

Damu sat up. Looking intently at her, he said, 'I've seen you somewhere, Miss Honavar. Do you recognize me?'

Geeta Honavar looked confused. She hadn't expected Damu or his question which was like a challenge.

'Ah, yes, I remember,' Damu went on, 'weren't you a patient last year at Dr. Jeevanlal Patel's hospital? I think you were to go through some kind of operation; I was chatting with Dr. Patel when you arrived.'

Geeta's face turned white, she began to tremble.

'Dr. Patel, Damu?'

'Ah, there is one, the well-known abortionist!'

'You are making a mistake.'

'I remember it distinctly,' said Damu, 'but never mind that. Will you have a drink? We've been drinking. One of us has retired. You see, we were arguing about what it means exactly when you say a woman has been raped. Our friend is a lawyer . . . .'

Geeta Honavar stood up and began to inch towards the door. Damu too got up and began to move towards her. She was terribly frightened.

'You are so luscious!' Damu said. 'Miss Honavar, you look very sexy.'

'Get away from me! Don't touch me!' she screamed, turning red and purple. 'I'm warning you . . . I'll complain to the police!'

'Easy, Miss Honavar; don't be nervous, Miss Honavar; see how uneasy you've made me!' Damu said as if he were reciting a poem.

'Drone . . . Drone . . . Drone . . . I'm a big male bee and you my lotus flower! I yearn to lie in the pollen bed of your pet'lous bower . . . .'

Geeta Honavar opened the door and stepping out, shut it with a bang.

'Shhh!' Damu said, hushing me up. 'Dipi, I think Lalita's gone to Antya's room.'

'Damn surprising!'

'What's so surprising about that? Antya must have her in his arms by now.'

'Holding her? He'd much rather be holding a brief for lawful behaviour. Surely, you don't expect him to be kissing a woman other than his wife?'

'But after all he's only made of flesh and blood, a man like you and me. Won't he give a proper welcome to a woman who's come on her own to him? Dipi, I think we should have a little more liquor. Is there some fleshy stuff that I could eat?'

'Fleshy? You'll find a chicken leg and a piece of pomfret on the table.'

Damu went off enthusiastically to the table. I sat on the sofa and emptied my glass, then lay on my side and fell asleep.

Damu shook me vigorously till I woke up. Antya was standing petrified by my side.

'Dipi! a ghastly thing has happened! Lalita has jumped down from the balcony! And she was naked!'

'O my God! How? When did it happen?'

'She was sleeping by my side — soundly. I was awake though. Then she woke up, stretched herself and said, I love all three of you; I shall become a man in my next life and you three can become women. And she promptly jumped down from the balcony!'

'It's going to be very difficult proving all this in court,' said Antya in a low voice. 'It's *finis* for the three of us.'

KASHI

ASHOK SRINIVASAN

nominated by Vijayalakshmi Quereshi

I have returned to Kashi with Paru, my daughter. I remember a song from my childhood, *First there was Kashi, then the world*. Later it was called Benaras. Now it is known as Varanasi. But I grew up here and for me it'll always be Kashi.

I know Paru yearns to be back with her old friends in Bombay, the city she grew up in. At eighteen years of age she burns with an intense beauty that was never her mother's when she was young. What young man, I wonder, will not be burnt to cinder at close contact with that unguarded face? I do not say this because she's my daughter. I do not say this because she is all I have. Like other girls of her age she will marry and leave me. That is as it should be. But I will not have her throw herself away on some riff-raff. When my wife deserted us, I said to myself, had the child been a boy or I the mother, things would have been different. Were I not a schoolmaster, with a daughter on my hands, I would have managed things better, more easily. I had got into the habit of arguing with myself. I don't as yet talk aloud to myself. Perhaps that too will happen. I used to keep telling myself these and similar things in such a way and to such an extent that I began to accept that things were as they were. Did I find new arguments to shift part of the burden off my shoulders and so console myself? Yes, yes. At any rate, those days I endlessly talked about these things to myself . . . .

I have returned to Kashi. Not because I wanted to revisit the scenes of my childhood or find easy access to the town's nightlife which I frequent out of boredom and which can hardly have more to offer than Bombay's redlight district, but because there seemed nowhere else to go. My wife suddenly turned up in Bombay, with a young man, after a twelve-year absence, and wanted to meet me in the teachers commonroom after school hours. I stared at them with the chalky fingers of my hands knitted in anger: my wife looked younger than I remembered and had the same helpless look, while the youth wore the face of a liar. She was a prostitute when I married her, against the combined opposition of my parents and all the relatives of the extended family. How could I then let them meet my Paru? Only my two friends stood by me: one of them is dead and the other (which is the same thing) has emigrated to America. I have not mentioned a word of all this to Paru. And so we came to Kashi, this city of cities.

My afternoons are free and I often take a walk down the shady side of the twisting streets; winters I sit out in the sun and read *Sports & Pastime*. Mornings, I teach at the Boys Normal School and evenings I hold special classes in non-formal adult education for which I've set apart a room in my house. I have the middle of the day all to myself as Paru goes off to the library directly after college and returns home only when I am taking my evening classes. I notice that we don't speak much to each other. Sometimes these special night-school classes are held in different parts of the city to enable those without any means of conveyance to attend them. On such and other nights Paru has a cup of hot tea ready for me when I enter the house, with my bicycle clips in one hand and the attendance register in the other. Sometimes she even helps me out with the maps and charts at the evening classes at home.

I've observed her on a Sunday morning, after a head bath, drying her long black hair at the window with a faraway look in her eyes. I never disturb her at such moments and take great care never to be caught watching her. But I know that look in her eyes though she does not say a word to me; she misses the city, the seaside and her old friends. The river banks at Kashi are crowded with beggars and believers. You don't have to beg or believe to walk among them. You are never part of the scene you see. And so it is with Paru. She longs for the lights of Bombay, its fast traffic and electric trains, and its magic anonymity of belonging to something that can never, in turn, belong to you. If she wants to return to Bombay I shall have to tell her about the incident in the school. But she says nothing and I don't explain.

One day I am offered the Deputy Headship. The following afternoon, just after the first rains, as I walk westwards through the Municipal Gardens past Gadaulia, I suddenly find myself behind the house I grew up in as a boy, looking down on it from a back street which is almost level with the roofs of row upon row of similar houses, several of them grouped into each compound. I don't remember them being here at all. Probably because it has rained all last night, the air vibrates with an aching clarity. It is the same old pile all right. Through the open doors of the hall I can see the jasmine bush on the front verandah; the open passage leading down to the central courtyard with the kitchen and lavatory on either side of the cowshed; and the well is in the centre, beside it the lemon tree whose branches overhang the unprotected staircase leading up to the four rooms opening into each other. My ancestral house is not located here at all. It's all wrong. My memory seems to be playing tricks on me. I grew up in an eastern suburb of Kashi. At all costs I must guard against the rising damp in my mind.

But my surprise at finding myself before my old home, or at finding it there, is nothing compared to the shock of seeing Paru leave the house through a side entrance and delicately make her way through the rubbish-strewn, narrow passage (where I played marbles as a child) towards the street that leads to town. I draw back involuntarily though I know that it is quite impossible for her to see me. Paru. My Paru.

It begins to drizzle and I don't know by what route I make my way back home. I only remember that as I'm leaving the place, the children in a neighbouring school are singing that maddening song, *First there was Kashi, then the world.* I retreat in wild confusion, my hands clapped to my ears.

Paru is not at home when I get back. There is an unopened envelope with the seal of the Chairman of the School Board waiting for me; it must be the formal letter informing me of my promotion. The first of my students, Srinivasan, an old man with a wheezing cough who comes in every day, is already waiting for me.

I let the letter lie unopened. We nod at each other in greeting.

As I towel my head dry I think that he comes to me for consolation, not education, for his stupidity is matched only by his regularity in attendance and his complaints about his emphysema. His lungs have long since lost their elasticity, he tells me; he seems to be waiting, after his fashion, for the end. There are worse places to die in than Kashi, even for a reprobate like myself. He will learn nothing here though he continues to hound me all my life.

'Let me see your copybook, please,' I say.

I give all my attention to Srinivasan for I do not want to think about Paru. I leaf through the blank pages; his roughbook is full of weak attempts at lewd drawings.

Poor devil! He used to be an itinerant quack performing cataract operations with a thorn on the eyes of unsuspecting villagers till the law caught up with him. He has a large family to support. And after the law caught up with him for the third time he set himself up as a faith-healer. He attends my classes only because the probationary officers require him to do so. In his studies he is exceptionally dense and in his work he must be, ailing as he is, the worst advertisement for his healing prowess, faith or no faith.

None of my other students come in and Srinivasan is fidgeting as if he would rather be elsewhere.

'Srinivasan,' I say, 'I know why you have to attend these classes. But as I've said before, you'll learn nothing here. I have promised to mark you present when you are absent and yet you turn up at all the night-school classes. You are the most regular even if the worst student in all of Kashi. It's a mystery to me.'

'I'll be frank with you,' he says. 'I'll be as frank with you as you have been with me. I'm not the man you take me for. I come to you simply because I've nowhere else to go. And now,' he says, getting to his feet, 'You'll have to excuse me. The other students have not turned up and will not turn up tonight. And I don't want to end up by saying things to you I should not as yet mention.'

I must somehow detain him. Even more, I'm intrigued and alarmed by his words and not untouched by his modest attempt at honesty.

'What is it that you cannot bring yourself to mention now to me?' I ask. I almost smile, in spite of myself, at these words.

'Would you recognise your master if you met him in the street?' he asks.

I must admit I'm quite unprepared for this. I cannot help grinning. 'My teacher or my maker?'

'It's nothing,' he mumbles and fussily gets out of the way of Paru who's at the door.

I have, however briefly, forgotten all about Paru. 'Don't go!' I cry, even though I don't want to see him any more; but he is gone and Paru holds my brown outstretched hand in both her own. The sudden contact — it is like in the old days when I used to take her for walks as a child, just after her mother had left us; and suddenly I realise that Paru has become the compass by which I take the bearings of my godless life.

'Father,' says Paru, leading me into the next room, 'I want you to meet Ashok.'

An abridged edition of that layabout Srinivasan. I look into the lying face of the young man standing before me, avoiding my eyes, much as he had stood before me all those years ago, with my wife by his side, in the school in Bombay.

'But Paru, he's a liar!' I almost say, but just in time I bite my tongue.

I see now that my wife is there sitting on the sofa. And so are a lot of others, among them my aunt and asthmatic uncle from Ghazipur, whom I've not seen in years.

If I look closely at the people gathered here I'm sure I should recognise all my old relations. But I don't have the time. And what is that idiot Srinivasan doing here? It is clear that they have met without me and have arrived at decisions that are now going to be put to me as accomplished facts. Who are these people and what are they to me? Where were they when I needed them? I never wanted them to meet my daughter. And because I want no part of them, I turn to Paru. I pull her back against the blackboard in the next room. My tone when I speak to her, though, is gentle. 'Paru, why have you deceived me?'

There is already the promise of tears in her voice when she says, 'Father you really must not give way to the feeling that I've betrayed you just because I want you to meet Ashok. One moment you are a god and the next you doubt your manhood. But look around you, father, sometimes. The world is changing. Where are you?'

'My child!' I say, 'I saw your mother with Ashok before you ever brought him to meet me.'

'It's a lie,' she cries, running out of the room.

Has somebody been talking to her about her mother's past? I see her whole future fading into her parents' past. The lying manipulators! Without visiting any violence on Paru I must teach them a lesson they will not forget. I'm not to be had in this way.

I return to the room and address my daughter who is standing, already composed, alone in a corner.

'Is this Ashok the man you want to marry, Parvati?' I ask, formally but clearly, in the sudden well of silence that my voice has created for itself amidst these people.

She hangs her head in the unmistakable sign of shy assent and the tears flow down her cheeks.

'All right, my child,' I say, and there are smiles all round and a general hubbub as though I have played my part exactly as they had arranged it for me. I turn my back on all that useless chatter and set out towards my childhood home where it all began. My life is in shambles now. I lose my way, retrace my steps and go through the Municipal Gardens, past Gadaulia . . . but it's no use. It's raining again. I must return home. But the house is nowhere to be seen. I rudely brush past an acquaintance with a new umbrella who stops me under a street lamp to exchange an amiable word or two with me.

My life here is finished. Full of resolution I take a taxi and give directions which will take me to the house situated on the other side of town as I remember it from childhood. And there in an eastern suburb of Kashi it stands in the dark exactly as I remember it, but now festooned with streamers, bunting, tinsel and paper-lanterns; the lemon tree is decorated with small winking lights and the lintels over the threshold and windows are trimmed with mango leaves; the cow and calf, their foreheads daubed with auspicious vermilion, are now tethered in front of the house, with a petromax gas-lamp for company.

As I enter the house I already know what I'll find. I'm now ready to accept whatever is decided for me.

There they are, all the people I had turned my back on at home. Ashok's father, Srinivasan — how could I have missed it earlier — ushers me into the room and introduces me to a bald, spare, nondescript man in ochre robes who smiles and says to me in the kindest tone, 'My brother,' as though he is continuing the conversation that he left off with Srinivasan, 'teaching, believing and learning have nothing to do with faith. It's only doing. Let me show you. You'll not regret it. Not for one moment.'

This is mere pious nonsense but I now have nothing to lose and do not argue, for I too now want to be taught the things that one never learns. I follow him out but turn back at the door to have one last look at these people: Paru is crying and next to her Ashok is at a loss, not knowing how to comfort her. Everybody is glum including my wife, as though things are going against their deepest desires. There is a smell of festive cooking in the air but the atmosphere is so heavy with gloom that I'm happy to leave them behind and follow this stranger. The sky has cleared and the breeze is picking up. In the moonlight I am made to sit on the stone steps of the ghats going down to the river and my head is shaved. After a dip in the dirty waters I'm smeared with sandalwood paste, anointed with holy oil and my forehead is marked with sacred ash and vermilion. I have returned to Kashi for this and this only.

I cast off my old clothes and instead receive two lengths of ochre cloth: one goes around my loins and the other is draped over my shivering shoulders; and in the weak light of the false dawn I start walking barefoot, with the new companion who is to accompany me: he is a young mute with a ready smile. First the Bishwanath Temple then the Manikarnika Kund and then south along the banks of the Ganga as far as the Assi Ghat, followed by prayers at the Durga Temple and so on to the Panchkosi Road, towards Kardameshwar, Bhimchadi, Rameshwar, Kapildhara, the Barna Sangam and so back to Manikarnika. The monsoon has started in earnest. I keep fasts, pray in Sanskrit, a language I do not know, and give alms from my share of the food. I bathe in the river everyday and invariably do as my brethren do. Time does not matter. To begin with I had to faithlessly repeat the words I never understood. The hours and years go by undifferentiated from each other in one continuous flow. By Ganga here I have laid down my burden in the holy city, eternal Kashi. Am I happy? Am I sad? May as well ask, am I alive? You beg, you believe, you belong.

THE ROOM BY THE TUBEWELL

SARAT KUMAR MUKHOPADHYAY

nominated and translated by
Enakshi Chatterjee

After a two-week rest in the intensive care unit, Shib Shankar Chakraborty's heart resumed its regular rhythm. The uneven triple beats stopped. His breathing became normal. For a man who had never known tender care or nursing, this was a heady experience. Full of gratitude he came back to his hospital ward to thank them all profusely.

This amused Gurupada, the lusty young village boy from Midnapur, lying in the next bed. His problem was a hole in the heart. His gasps came out in whistles, very much like the sound rubber dolls give out when you squeeze them. Since his village hospital did not have the means for treating this kind of ailment,

'Kaltalar Pasher Ghar' ('The Room by the Tubewell') was first published in Bangla in *Jugantor*, 1988.

he was in the city. This visit happened to be his third. Only this time, it would be a longer stay because they were going to mend the hole — a major operation, they said.

'Much bigger than Operation Barga,' Gurupada smirked. His black lower lip parted from the upper, revealing an interior just as black, like the mouth of a crow. This was probably the result of long years of bidi smoking. Now of course, there was no question of smoking.

'You know what . . .' said Gurupada, 'you know what I think of these doctors? A bunch of novices — the whole lot! Not enough guts. And the gang leader is busy looking after his own interests — he has no time for others. The fellow wouldn't even give a date, keeps putting it off. And here I'm bent double with all this croaking and cawing.' His long stay in the hospital had made him bitter. 'How is it that you are here?' He was curious. 'Whose reference got you in?'

Shib Shankar said, 'I don't know about any references. I was getting off the tram when I had a blackout. The people around me were kind. They brought me here. One of them may have known somebody, but I'm completely in the dark.'

'Let me tell you something brother,' said the wordly-wise Gurupada. 'You have nothing to be thankful for. These air-conditioned rooms, they are not really meant for the likes of you or me. They are for the machines. The machines will start barking if there is a speck of dust inside — that is why they are so finicky about cleanliness. Besides . . .' he moved the red blanket from his legs and smiled mischievously, 'a couple of days' stay in the Intensive is enough to turn your heart to jelly.'

Shib Shankar did not quite comprehend the significance of Gurupada's words. He did, however, a couple of days later. On Wednesday morning the ward boy summoned him upstairs to the

Operation Barga: The reference is to the CPM movement in the 1970s, involving the transfer of land to landless labourers. The phrase has since become part of common Bangla vocabulary.

senior doctor's chamber. The boy did not leave him there but took the trouble of escorting him up the lift.

Dr. Choksi examined his papers. 'So, you are all right now,' he said.

'Yes, sir.'

'We are going to release you. But you must be careful.'

'Yes, sir.'

'You must take the medicines I prescribe. Take them regularly. Come for a check-up every six months. Understand?'

'A check-up! Again?'

'Well, a weak heart is a pretty serious matter. It's not like malaria or typhoid that a course of medicine will cure you. This is a vital organ, the pumping station of the body so to say, working non-stop. Your beats have slipped — they are not rhythmic.'

'But now they are back to the regular rhythm, sir.'

Dr. Choksi looked a little annoyed. 'They may go out of rhythm any time — life is full of tension and there's so much pollution in Calcutta!'

At last Shib Shankar Chakraborty mustered up enough courage to declare, 'But sir, there is no tension in my life.'

For the first time the doctor actually looked at Shib Shankar. He saw before him not Shib Shankar but Shibram Chakraborty, the almost legendary Bengali humorist — a round chubby face, a silk kurta — a life without tension. He asked several probing questions and found that Shib Shankar's claim to a tension-free life was quite justified.

If one can visualise the area between Howrah and Sealdah, keeping Mahatma Gandhi Road in the centre, like the bones of a pomfret, then Harihar Sau Lane would be the seventeenth spike from the fish-head. This is where Shib Shankar lived. The lane meandered, changed its name a number of times before joining the spacious Vivekananda Road. Between Mahatma Gandhi and Vivekananda lies a multi-ethnic slum. There is a single tubewell to provide water for the entire slum population. For the last thirty-three years Shib Shankar has been living in a room just two houses away from the tubewell.

Thirty-three years! This part of Calcutta has not changed one bit in the last thirty-three years. There used to be a crooked palm tree near the entrance to his room but with time it has withered, leaving unhindered his line of vision to the tubewell. Poets and rhymesters have waxed eloquent about their lovers drawing water from a well or a tank; Shib Shankar drew inspiration from this tubewell in his own way, not like Chandidas had done from the village pond and certainly not like Shibram Chakraborty may have done.

Once or twice during the day he went indoors, into the interior of the building teeming with people who had occupied it by force. He finished his work which did not involve interaction with others. He did not talk to anyone either. This had been his life for the last thirty-three years.

He had no wife, no children, no property and no domestic help. He had neither a kitchen nor a toilet, no car, no job. He had no friends, no enemies, and no ambition. It was a tension-free life. He roamed around in the book-publishing para*, correcting proofs. That was his livelihood and it was enough to keep him going.

He was very young when the country gained independence. He had run away from home, drawn by the charms of Calcutta. There was a time when he hawked just about everything — newspapers, Tansen tablets, bed-bug eliminators, dhoop. He learnt the hard way that in order to earn two rupees you have to do a five-rupee job — three rupees went to the employer. Gradually he lost interest in this sort of work. Cheating people can also be a means of livelihood. For some time he worked as an assistant to an astrologer. His job was to make amulets, clean the Kali image and brush the marble Mahadeb. But he did not like the job and could not stick to

The neighbourhood around College Street in North Calcutta where most of the local publishers have their offices.

it. The pandit had a way of swindling his clients — he never charged a fat fee for himself, but the list of things to be brought was always long: bundles of red-bordered saris, gamchas, brass pots, jars and lamps — these items circulated back and forth, from him to the client and back to him again. He even went to the length of melting Kali's gold tongue and bangles to make ornaments for his second wife. He suspected Shib Shankar of pinching money from the box of offerings. The pandit-astrologer did not have any peace of mind himself, poor fellow.

Shib Shankar has seen enough of this heartless city — its many faces. The city does not inspire love. People exploit it for their pleasure and later use it as a garbage bin. People react violently at the slightest provocation. They say that the city was not like this before. The pressure of population since Partition has been responsible for the city's loss of character. However that may be, Shib Shankar remained a resident of the city.

He pays eleven rupees as room rent. The cost of food has gone up; it now costs him two hundred and fifty a month. Since he has no regular job, he has no real transport expenses. He walks to work and goes to the park for a breath of free air. When he feels like it, he takes a tram ride. This much money he is obliged to earn. He never falls sick — no expense on that account. This was the first time he was ill.

He has never consciously done any good to others. Has carefully kept out of all protest movements, even processions. Such things are not his business. He has never paid any subscription for pujas, nor ever donated a drop of blood. The local boys bully others for the various community pujas, but Shib Shankar is left alone. Even the beggars avoid him like poison. Everyone knows him well.

So much is happening all over the world but none of it bothers Shib Shankar. He doesn't read newspapers, not in the accepted sense, that is. He reads old newspapers bought by the kilo, and having read them, sells them off again. But for one exception, he has never harmed anyone in his life. That was a long time ago.

A girl used to come to the tubewell towards late morning for her bath, a gamcha round her waist, swinging a tin bucket. Nobody came so late, because by then the flow of water was reduced to a trickle. She took a long time bathing. She held in her teeth one end of the sari, showing off her body — and her curves — to Shib Shankar. Shib Shankar sat very still, his eyes seemingly glued to the old newspapers. The girl exposed her legs, flipped her wet hair noisily, lifted the sari up to her thighs as she dried herself. All the while, a smile played on her lips, although she carefully kept her face turned the other way.

This went on for some time. One day Shib Shankar beckoned her. 'Come here, Ruli.'

She hesitated at first. Then she obliged, prompted partly by familiarity, partly by an unspoken understanding. She came up to the door and asked, 'Yes?'

'Come inside, then I'll tell you.'

She came in. Shib Shankar carefully closed the door but did not lock it.

He said, 'Take off your wet clothes. Let me have a proper look, you've been showing me parts of yourself for so long.'

'Oh come on,' she said, but did not move. Perforce Shib Shankar had to peel off her clothes, one by one, the sari first, then the blouse, then the petticoat. He drew out her body much in the same way as a fisherman takes out fish from the meshes of his net. The body of a woman looked kind of formless, even ugly, to him. You can't look at any other place except the face and the feet. The rest is hideous — like a worm.

Ruli was kneeling on the floor breathing heavily, too embarrassed to stand or to look at Shib Shankar.

This perhaps was a woman's shame. Only once does she feel shame — the first time she exposes herself before a man. She would never again feel shame, thought Shib Shankar. For the rest of her life she would know only lust. That was unfortunate. He felt sorry for her. He was responsible for this unintended harm to her. Then he forgot all about the incident.

Before leaving Ruli had asked him, 'Will you marry me?'

'Yes, yes, of course, but you must grow up a bit.' He slipped a one-rupee coin into her palm. 'All in good time.'

Ruli kept coming to the tubewell to take her bath as she had always done, flipped her hair dry, filled the bucket with water and went back home. She never looked his way again. Damned liar — she must have thought. But never spoke to him about it. She grew up, and then probably got married or moved away with her family. Shib Shankar, not interested any more, did not bother to keep track.

Today, when he had told the doctor that he suffered from no tension, obviously this incident was not bothering his conscience.

Dr. Choksi drummed a beat on the table for some time. Then he said, 'Put in a pacemaker. Then you won't have to worry.'

'A pacemaker? What is that?'

'It is a device — small, like a wrist watch. It is inserted under the skin. It ticks away along with the heart and corrects the heart if the beats go wrong. People go all over the place with a pacemaker inside them — to Delhi, to Madhupur.'

'Is that so?'

He had no desire to be immortal, neither was he keen on dying too soon. He had no family, no ambition, no job, no friend or foe. He had been in this hospital for the last two weeks, but nobody came to see him.

Nobody, except one person. He was Hanuman Prasad, the Hindustani hawker who sold vegetables and slept under a portico on Vivekananda Road. He was not allowed in by the hospital staff when Shib Shankar was in the Intensive Care. But they wrote down his name. The face was quite familiar. In all likelihood he was around when Shib Shankar fell getting off the tram. Perhaps he was one of the group who brought him to the hospital. Perhaps it was Hanuman Prasad who had given them his address.

'Are you thinking of the expenses involved?' Asked Dr. Choksi.
'That's right, sir.'

'It would cost around fifteen thousand.'

'Where would I get all that money, sir? I have nobody, I have
nothing. But if I can live for ten more years with the help of this
instrument, then I'll pay you back by monthly instalment. You
should not suffer any loss on my account. I wouldn't want that, sir.
That wouldn't be fair.'

'Why are you under the impression that you are all alone in this
world? You do have a wellwisher who is willing to pay for it. I've
had a talk with him.'

'Who could that be — Hanuman Prasad? Is he the one? But why
should he part with so much money for my sake?'

'Search me,' laughed the doctor. 'It takes all kinds to make this
world. What do you know of that! He'll come again, you better talk
to him.'

A month and a half later, the people of the neighbourhood saw
Shib Shankar being helped out of a taxi by Hanuman Prasad. The
taxi drew right up to his room. It was around ten-thirty in the
morning. The neighbours assembled at the tubewell watched with
amusement the locked door being opened after a long time. The old
familiar figure — nobody knew him by name — chubby face, silk
kurta, walked up to his cot and sat down. Hanuman Prasad took
up the broom and started sweeping the floor.

It is difficult to fool the neighbours. They know exactly what
transpires when an unmarried girl disappears to come back after a
few months. They know that she has had an abortion. You don't
have to tell them. A man coming home after a vasectomy is at once
identified by the foolish smile stuck on his face. No wonder then
that the residents, particularly the young men of Harihar Sau Lane,
came to know about the pacemaker in no time. One had to be very
rich in order to afford that sort of an ornament. It was clear that this
man who lived in one room, never parted with his money or blood,
never gave anything to a beggar or to boys collecting subscription,

was actually a deep one. He had money stashed away somewhere — quite a lot of it. That is why he could wear a pacemaker
on his heart and keep Hanuman Prasad as his servant and manage
to acquire such a glowing look.

That was how it appeared to outsiders.

Shib Shankar slept on the cot. Hanuman Prasad spread a mat on
the floor for himself; sometimes a rug over the mat. The room was
on the ground floor and quite damp. No sunlight came in. Shib
Shankar felt ill at ease, knowing that he was up to his ears in debt.

He said to Hanuman Prasad, 'You spent the money for nothing.
Who knows when I'll die. You'll be an old man by the time you get
possession of this room. And your wife will be wasting away in the
village.'

'For god's sake, babu. Don't say that. I am in no hurry.'

'You would have had a much better return if you had invested
the money in business.'

'By your grace, I now have a roof over my head, babu. Let me
have the pleasure of serving a Brahmin at least for some time.'

People passing by, the residents of the slum taking their bath,
saw Hanuman Prasad cook in a corner of the room. He no longer
went about with the basket on his head but sat by the stairs selling
his goods. He kept stationery and grocery on a shelf inside the
room.

Shib Shankar hardly left the cot, he just sat reading old newspapers. It seemed like he lived in comfort but inwardly he felt
miserable. The burden of gratitude weighed heavy. The pacemaker
had become a symbol of his misery. He had no desire to live. He
was fifty-six, what was the use of living any longer?

He felt grateful but not repentant. After all these years he
recalled the Ruli incident, how he had stripped her, how he
brought her naked body out of her clothes, taking them off one by
one. Was the body ugly? Not really. He had touched her at various
places but he couldn't recall any of those sensations. He had put
his finger into her ears to take the water out — the action shook her

tits which looked like dark plums. He did not rape or molest her in any way. All he did was to divest her of shame. Will you marry me she had asked.

He felt bad about it now. It hurt, the deep feeling of remorse. This was a new development — feelings of guilt, repentance, gratefulness. It had all started with the insertion of the pacemaker. It was a costly thing, made in USA. Stainless steel body, bound in goat skin, not a cheap thing of plastic. The watch was electronic. The costly pacemaker has made up for all the drawbacks of his heart.

Men can survive pollution or tension. But they cannot live once the will to live is gone. All those who die natural deaths, die because they have lost the lust for life. All the guilt, repentance, old memories, the thought of what could have happened but did not — all these are like the police car with its siren shrieking and lights blinking, behind which the Chief Minister's car glides noiselessly.

One day the Chief Minister's car reached Harihar Sau Lane. It came early in the morning. Hanuman Prasad awoke to find his babu scratching the closed door, trying to open the lock, as happens very often in the case of heart patients. Then he dropped like a lump.

Hanuman Prasad put the body on the floor and rushed to Dr. Choksi and brought him. It was not clear if the doctor was surprised to see the room but he took it well. Wrote out the death certificate and said, 'I am sorry Hanuman. Don't break down. This is all a part of life. You have to take the ups with the downs.' He did not wait for his fees, and left even before Hanuman Prasad could ask him if the machine was a fake.

When Panchanan the rikshawala arrived at the tubewell, brushing his teeth with a neem twig, he saw Shib Shankar's door shut and Hanuman Prasad sitting on the doorstep, weeping.

In no time a crowd gathered. They all had a few tears to shed for this man who was a familiar sight, reading newspapers and looking at the tubewell. His name was not known to them but nevertheless, he was a neighbour. He never talked to anyone but that did not stop them from expressing grief. Too bad he did not live even for a couple of years after having the costly pacemaker put inside him.

There was no need to inform anyone. At the right moment Chamu, the acknowledged leader of the para turned up with his four friends. They had brought a cot, some flowers, dhoop and incense, thinking there would be nobody to claim the body. But Hanuman Prasad paid for everything. Moreover he handed Chamu the death certificate and a hundred-rupee note. 'Keep this babu, you'll need it. I can't go myself. But please see that he has a proper cremation — he was such a pious man.'

'Okay, okay.' Chamu was impatient. He and his friends lifted the body and rushed towards Vivekananda Road hollering out the 'Hari bol.' It was office time: the traffic had picked up.

Before reaching Rabindra Sarani, Chamu yelled, 'Put the body down.' It was a long way to the ghat. Perhaps a little rest was needed. But Chamu was bothered by another thought. A doctor, at any cost. They must get a surgeon. Even a dentist would do. This body has a brand new pacemaker inside. It must be taken out before the body is put on the pyre.

No surgeon was ready to oblige them. Finally they threatened a dentist into doing what they wanted. They carried the body to his chamber and put it on the padded chair, even though it was a corpse. After all an operation is an operation. The dentist sterilised his instruments, got them ready for the operation. 'He was about to vanish with goods worth fifteen thousand!' remarked Chamu. 'Made in USA — the sly fox. If it's inside, it will explode like a bomb.'

With six pair of eyes watching intently, the cloth was removed. It revealed a freshly stitched cut by the side of the old scar. Bits of raw flesh peeped through the hastily done stiches.

'Sala Hanuman Prasad!' Chamu sprang up in anger.

But what was the point? By that time, the culprit was on the Mithila Express on his way to Muzaffarpur. He would lie low for some time and then attend to the needs of his farm. He planned to bring his family to Calcutta after a while — one room to begin with, then another, and another.

As he thought of the possibilities his head began to swim.

PRAKASINI'S CHILDREN

SARA JOSEPH

nominated and translated by
Ayyappa Paniker

Prakasini dipped into the small circle of greenish water surrounded by African weeds. She raised her head, wiped the slime trickling down her eyelids and she dipped again. Once ... Twice ... Thrice .... After the seventh dip she climbed out of the pond. Transparent green filament covered her body; flowers of the African weed clung to her tangled hair. There were little fishes in the cup of her navel. Parrots flew down from the bamboo cluster and squatted on her shoulders. Crickets and grasshoppers frisked about her toes ....

Prakasini bowed to the sun above. She bent to kiss the earth. She saluted water, air and sky. Then, raising palms pressed into each

Prakasiniyude Makkal ('Prakasini's Children'), was first published in Malayalam in *Mathrubhumi Weekly*, September 24-30, 1989.

other, she received the touch of the five elements on every limb.

Her father, walking down the steps of the pond to wash his face, was shocked to see the naked girl standing like a statue sculpted out of black granite. It took him a minute to recover. Then, he screamed out to the mother, his hand on his chest . . . Why was the girl's belly so swollen?

Amma was scouring the milkpot in the kitchen when she heard Acchan's cry. Startled, she got up to run towards the pond. After her came Mutthassi, Prakasini's grandmother, and trailing her, the servants and domestic animals. Acchan stood speechless, his finger pointing towards the pond.

Amma saw the full figure of the girl, her body smeared with sunlight and turmeric. She shuddered to see the bulging buttocks that refused to be covered by the heavy flowing tresses. Mutthassi gaped at the full rounded breasts, the widening dark blue circles around the nipples. The servants and domestic animals put fingers on their noses. Look at that belly rounded like a folk musician's drum-pot, their eyes mocked.

'Prakasini!' Amma looked as if she were willing her eyes to pierce into her daughter's abdomen and discover its secret. She shook her daughter's body.

Like a flower unfolding its petals, Prakasini opened her eyes. Then she stepped into the pond again — knee-deep, waist-deep, breast-deep, neck-deep in water — her hands raised above her head, her face beaming.

'Has my child gone mad?' Mutthassi cried out, her hands on her head. 'What's happened to her? Has she seen something and taken fright?'

The maids muttered amongst themselves, their fingers still touching the tips of their noses.

Her eyes flaming, Amma drove the servants away. Then, 'Prakasini, my child!' she called softly.

'Come away here to me, child,' Mutthassi begged.

Prakasini did not hear them. She did not see them.

'A beating is what she needs. No use being soft . . . playacting after such a shameful deed!' Amma was furious. She ran down the steps, grabbed her daughter by the hair and dragged her along.

The parrots in the bamboo jungle flew up in a wild flutter. Rattles and hisses rose from the palaces of nagathan.

Prakasini came away, a nipped waterlily.

'Girl, she's carrying!' Mutthassi's palsied hands stopped Amma.

But nothing could stop Prakasini's mother. She dragged her daughter up the steps and across the bamboo grove to lock her up in a storeroom with no air or light. Outside sat Acchan, his hands and feet paralysed.

Mutthassi stroked Prakasini's face with her icecold fingers. 'Who deceived you my child? Who?'

Prakasini felt like laughing. She was reminded of the white lily in bloom near the eastern side of the pond. Siddhartha and Syamala are the children of the white waterlily, Prakasini said.

'Kesava! Bring her a holy thread consecrated with mantra. My child has got a fright.' Tears dropped every now and then from Mutthassi's eyes.

In the storeroom where no air and light ever enter, Prakasini lay, her heart full of light. The hail of questions never touched her. She did not know their heat or sharpness. What she knew and remembered was something else. *Prakasini, we shall live through several births, as Siddhartha, as Syamala . . . .*

They were making love, pressing hard on the tender grass growing on the hillside. From her body arose the scent of the newly-ploughed earth. He smelled of the rains of July. The hillside echoed with the discordant music of green foliage and little birds. Out of their love they wanted to bring forth Siddhartha and Syamala.

But the noise from the valley did not let them stay.

Mushrooms of fire sprouted like umbrellas and burst into the air all along the hillside.

Fire and smoke came sizzling towards them.

The bed of green grass crackled and burnt.

The sulphurous air thickened and choked them.

Frightened by the bombs that seemed to burst wherever feet touched earth, he dragged her and ran towards the valley. Rushing down, she asked, 'You too had joined them to sow the mushroom seeds?'

He stopped, shuddering. He had gone to sow the mushrooms so that she could eat them and recover her health after the birth of Siddhartha and Syamala.

Dark red clouds gathered over their heads. A drop of blood tasting of salt stung Prakasini's lower lip. Prakasini looked fearful. 'Are they not to be born at all?' she asked.

He wiped her lip with his pale trembling fingers. 'No Prakasini,' he cried out, 'not here! Let us not be reborn here.'

A wind rose somewhere on the slopes of the hill. It covered their faces and hair and their bodies with burnt grass. He looked as if he lay on his funeral pyre, covered with ash. The tender grass, the heart-warming rain that waters them — will they not be born again? 'Wait! We must give birth to Siddhartha and Syamala!' she cried till she was exhausted.

He took her on his shoulders. They wandered on the slopes looking for a place to create Siddhartha and Syamala till they reached the end of the long line in the valley, where mothers waited for their turn with empty tins, their faces covered with rags.

They were tired. Very tired. All they needed was a bed of grass.

The mothers pointed to rooms that had been reduced to ashes where hungry, weeping children lay heaped together. Where the faeces and urine and death of children fought for space, there was no room for adults.

Yet, they lay down in the small space created by pressing the children against themselves.

Outside, it was a festival of fire mushrooms. Shouts and wails mingled with blood that fell like rain. Dogs of hunger carried off children from the ash heap. The child that lay next to them was dying. It was a night of terror. They made love trembling with fear . . . .

When she woke up he wasn't there. She could feel Syamala and Siddhartha quicken inside her. Where could he be?

Stepping over the dead child, crossing the lines of mothers still waiting for their turn, she rushed to the hillside in search of him, feeling her love for him boiling within her.

Their hill had turned into little heaps of cinder. The wind hung a veil of ash over her eyes. Eagle-eyed, she searched for her lover. Where is he? Where is he? Lost like a blade of grass in the womb of the earth?

In the dark cellar someone pulls open a ventilator. Someone ties a mantric thread on Prakasini's right wrist. Someone pours holy water on her face. Someone whispers, 'The honour that is gone is gone. Better now to hush things up before people come to know of it.'

Prakasini stares, looks dazed. She is lying on her back on a grassmat spread on the floor. Before her, like a hill stands a chami who kills enemies with the magical drug made from the foetuses of first pregnancies. His eyes burn like cinders. His teeth shine like silver.

'Leave her! Quit!' the Chami recites. 'This was not sown by common consent. You must quit! Let the womb be clean.'

Prakasini was overpowered by the strong smell of the herbal mixture that was being circled round her head and thrown at her face accompanied by chanting. She sank into bottomless depths. Her feet slipped and felt unsteady. Hairy hands smeared with magic herbs encircled her bulging belly. Hot fingertips came searching for her womb.

Prakasini shook them off. Bit off Amma's hands which rushed to hold her back. Scratched and tore Acchan's face. Sprang up to gouge out the eyes and heart of the magician, turning her thin pale fingers into a trishulam.

'Are my children to blame?' Prakasini roared at them.

The worm-eaten pillars of the large house shook.

'I will kill!' muttered Acchan.

Striking her head on the blackened kitchen wall, Amma said brokenly, 'I am dying! I don't want to live. I won't live after this loss of honour.'

Someone is leaving with a twisted bundle of strong-smelling green herbs that have proved quite useless. The clatter of instruments that have had no effect on Prakasini descends down the front steps.

Prakasini strokes her abdomen with relief. What is an oyster shell for, Siddhartha? she asks silently. Syamala, what is an oyster shell for?

Siddhartha and Syamala responded from within her womb, hurting her like two sand particles.

Fondly stroking Prakasini's face, Mutthassi called her. 'Child? Who is it that deceived you? Why don't you say something? Tell me, child, and we'll bring him here.'

Pressing her face into Mutthassi's cold hands, Prakasini remembered . . . .

Prakasini, he will be my heir. I will hand over my infinite riches to him. My wet lands, palaces, art treasures, servants, horses, laboratories, ammunition stores. Everything will be his. I'll teach him how to look after them and keep them.

He had said these words with his ear on her abdomen.

Prakasini's whole body was like a cyclone let loose to bind him to her. But now there was no hillside for them to lie on. There were only heaps of ashes instead of love-endorsing grass. She was afraid of mating like dogs on an ash heap.

Prakasini mourned, unable to control her shaking thighs, 'Give me a place to lie down. A little space with green grass. A little bit of the blue sky. A small stream . . . .'

'Prakasini, I have all this in my airconditioned room. Green and gold, and a cool breeze. There we can love forever.' From the dry machines came the song of brooks and its cool breeze caressed them. 'Give me a son. My heir.'

He fondled her belly. But Prakasini could only ask, 'How did you come by these airconditioned rooms?'

Once he had been poor.

He didn't answer her question. 'Prakasini, we now have airconditioned rooms. Why do we need hillsides, fields of grass, jungles?'

Prakasini's love froze. Her thighs grew stiff. She would not give birth to Siddhartha and Syamala for them to become masters of airconditioned rooms. Their destiny lay elsewhere.

Stroking her pale, gloomy face and letting her lean on his shoulders he led her out. He felt sad that she still preferred hillsides and fields. They walked silently through the smouldering ash heaps. He continued to stroke her belly. 'Prakasini, speak to me about my children,' he said with great eagerness.

'They are the children of the sun,' she said lazily, leaning on him. She was thirsty, carrying with her two rays of the sun. 'They are the children of this mountain, of the trees, of the rivers, of the seas, of the stars . . . .'

Prakasini never said anything without a purpose. Crushing her body fiercely he said, 'You cannot prove this.'

Prakasini burst out laughing, 'I alone can prove it.'

He knelt down before her. 'Prakasini, my endless wealth, my rice fields, laboratories, ammunition stores, soldiers . . . don't they need an heir?' He drew Siddhartha close to him by force.

At that moment she understood that she had to give birth to his enemies. She left him behind and walked away. She joined the long line of mothers waiting for their turn with empty tins. She begged to be given a place where she could give birth to her children.

'How can you give birth to your children here? Where can we find a labour room? You know there is no space here. Grass will not grow on this soil. There is not a drop of water. We don't have vegetables or even weeds . . . Prakasini, you have seen the ash house where children crying with hunger have been packed in layers. You know there is no space for two more children.'

The mothers showed their empty tins held upside down and pointed out the children growing in numbers and spilling over. Hiding their faces with rags they said harshly, 'It is a sin to bring them here, Prakasini.'

Prakasini wept.

She wept silently. Mutthassi's cold fingers burned when her tears fell on them. Her mind too burned. 'My child! O my child, people will say you had a child the wrong way . . . .'

Prakasini sat up. 'Mutthassi, I need a small patch of ploughed land to give birth.'

Mutthassi started and drew back.

Prakasini's eyes shine like stars. She has no doubt that Siddhartha and Syamala will come. They have to come. She'll bring them to life in July, the season of unending rain.

Prakasini needs a plough to turn up the soil and prepare the ground on the hillside where the trees grow thick. When the children come into this world, she needs the July rains to wash them. It is the scent of soaked earth and wet leaves that they should first breathe. Their hearts should beat to the sound of thunderbolts. It is the music of the wind and the rain that they should first hear. It is the colour of the sky that they should first see. It is the salt of the sea that they should first taste . . . .

They are the children of Prakasini.

DREAM IMAGES

SURENDRA PRAKASH

nominated by Anisur Rahman
translated by M. Asaduddin

That day, I burnt my fingers as I touched the newspaper. Every item of news was an ember. Outside, one could hear a rattling noise, the kind made by moving tanks. There is the danger of an immediate war with Pakistan.

We have already fought three wars with Pakistan. These sporadic wars, each lasting for several days, cast their shadows on the doors, windows and kitchens of our houses. During those dark years I got my elder daughter married. She is happy in her home with a little darling of a son. I have come by many such things which I thought I did not deserve. In my own way I am contented with my life.

'Khayal Surat' ('Dream Images') was first published in Urdu in *Zehn-e-Jadeed*, September–November, 1990.

I think I have separated myself from society, but as I read the newspaper I feel at one with it and the whole situation undergoes a change. Thoughts get blurred. Embers continue to burn.

It is unaesthetic to talk about inflation, homelessness or a feeling of insecurity, and anything, any sort of behaviour which is unaesthetic is abhorrent to me. Yet, I remember how the country was divided because of the conflict between two religions. According to a preconceived scheme we were thrown out lock, stock and barrel from the place which has become Pakistan to this side. And many Muslim families from here proceeded towards their new heaven.

I was then a child, but I kept thinking why we had to be either Hindu or Muslim. The answer lay in our birth — because we were born of parents who were either Hindu or Muslim. We were Hindu. So we could not retain even two yards of land in Pakistan. Those of us who survived, came to India. The only things which remained there were memories and shadows. Master Nazir Talib remained there and so did Akhtar Bhai; Jalal Painter was there and so was our neighbour Meraj Sheikh, the shopkeeper. All of them were Muslims. They were born to families which were Muslim before their birth. Nevertheless there must be something common between us that makes me think about them so often.

The Muslims migrating from here did not leave *en masse*. No one knows what logic made them divide their families. The pain of truncated families must haunt them even today. I have been lucky. Coming here I have found my own Nazir Talib, Akhtar Bhai, Jalal Painter, Mirza and Meraj Sheikh in Mehmood Javed, Zubair, Anwar and Salam. Alas, what would have happened to those who went there from here?

The day moved on, slowly. With the newspaper hugged to my chest I lay on the bed littered with embers. And then, I don't know when, my eyes closed.

'. . . You have done a good thing.'

Startled, I looked at my wife who had said these words. We were sitting together on the back seat.

'What?' I asked.

'You've brought the children along!'

I looked at my son and younger daughter who were sitting next to the driver. They were talking to each other in hushed tones, perhaps about the place we were going to. The car was one of those big, ancient chevrolets. The driver's face looked young though his beard and moustache were perfectly white.

'I've always dreamt of doing this. The timing too is perfect,' I said. 'You may put it down to my age.'

'Hmm. Tell me, have you even thought of how I'd live without you or you without me, in such a world?'

The car sped along and we could see everything in front of us through the windscreen. Now I could see bushes along the road, of a kind we hadn't passed earlier. It was dusty all around and the colours were exactly as I remembered them. The wind was raging. It had an aroma of its own. The stems of kekar and tehli were swinging in the strong wind. I couldn't come up with an answer to my wife's question. Only a supernatural power could have answered it.

We passed by the burning ghat, by Adh Marg where all the water taps were running. Behind Adh Marg we could see hamlets spread out for long stretches. When we reached the bridge on the canal, the car slowed down. We passed the bridge and entered the market where the car came to a stop on the left. I was the first to get out. I saw Babaji's temple standing there just as it had before. Outside, under a peepul tree, some sadhus were sucking at a chillum, letting out deep puffs of smoke through their mouths and noses. They had tangled hair, their bodies were smeared with bhabhut and they wore just a piece of cloth. Near them were cows lazily chewing the cud.

I turned to look across the market and saw the clock in the clocktower but could not see its hands. The market was very crowded. I tried to remember its name but couldn't. I also couldn't recall the name of the mohalla near which we stood. Yet, I was sure that it was the very same mohalla where our house used to be.

The driver took out the luggage from the car and my wife paid the fare. The two children looked around with surprise. They looked at me as though to ask: What next, Daddy?

'Right here, behind these shops, was our home,' I said without much thought.

'Come on, let's have a look,' all the three said in unison.

We shared the luggage amongst ourselves and set off. There were thousands of people moving around us, whose faces were invisible. Bodies moving with clothes on. Begging bowl in hand, one of the followers of Baba Kaudi Shah passed by us, nodding his head and begging for alms. Such begging bowls used to be brought from the faraway island of Madagascar. They were made by ripping open a fruit that looked like a watermelon. Three bowls from a single fruit. Several generations could use the same bowl for begging.

We entered the mohalla. The street and the houses alongside them looked the same. Several houses had come up in the open space in front of the mohalla changing the entire topography. We could not stand for long in front of our ancestral home. Too many eyes stared at us from behind the walls.

All of a sudden I saw Babuji coming out of the house, ready for his daily walk to the shop. Ma came up to the threshold to see him off.

'Who was that, Daddy?' both my children asked me.

'Your Dadaji and Dadiji.'

My wife joined her palms in a namaskar from a distance. 'How fortunate we are that we could have a darshan of our ancestors!' she said in a whisper as though she were reciting verses from the Quran.

'Where is Dadaji going, Daddy?' my children asked me once again.

'To his shop.'

'Where is his shop?'

'Come, let's find out.'

We had left the street and had moved on to Gol Bagh just behind Regal Cinema. Then we passed through Changadh and Badru. We saw the shrine of Baba Kaudi Shah where dervishes were ecstatically chanting,

> *Ali da, mast qulandar,*
> *Ali da, Ali da mast qulandar*

They were swinging their heads from side to side while the disciples of Shah Dauley observed them intently, their own heads beginning to move. Clutching their begging bowls, the disciples tried to steady their heads. But in vain. The heir to the shrine, dressed in black, his hair unkempt, gazed at the dome with his bright and beautiful eyes. Then, muttering to himself, he bowed his head and tried to hold it between his knees. The pigeons perched on the dome did not stir.

My children watched all this for quite some time, completely absorbed in it till my wife said, 'Children, say Allah, Allah.' They joined their palms and said 'Allah, Allah,' as though they were praying before the images of gods.

Far away, the clock in the tower chimed the noon hour. Kites flying in the sky let out a cry. A handcart selling malai qulfi, drawn by four identical-looking brothers, went past us. They sang out together,

> *Qulfi khoye-malai di, piste badam di,*
> *keode qulab di, khatir janab di . . . .*

In a huge wooden box the qulfi moulds were stabbed into the ice. A white sheet was spread over them. The box was painted light green, the borders deep green. On them was written, 'Abdus Shakur and Sons, Qulfiwaley,' in black.

The four of us bought a qulfi each and sucked it. It was great fun. I said, 'The eyes are moist, the heart is soothed.'

My wife and children also put on expressions of contentment on their faces. The cart moved along.

We threw away the sticks on the road that leads to Regal Cinema. We followed the road which stretched ahead of us. Soon there appeared a high dome. There was a desolate temple. Sitting on a platform, some people dressed in white dhotis and shirts were talking to each other in low voices. One of them thrust his hand inside his shirt. Putting the other hand under his collar he caught hold of his sacred thread and started pulling it up and down so that it became a convenient device for scratching his back. In the ruins in front of the temple there stood a newly-built dharamshala. Vendors has stationed themselves near its doors and were selling food. The atmosphere was strangely quiet.

We put our luggage down with a sense of relief and looked around. A man who was scratching his beard came close to us and said, smiling, 'Welcome to the Hindu dharamshala. You can stay here.'

It was a happy occasion. Having lived as unwanted tenants in other people's houses all our lives, here at last was a welcome invitation.

'Thank you. We shall stay here,' I said with pleasure and relief. My wife agreed with me.

'Daddy,' my daughter said, 'Why have we come here?'

My wife and I looked at each other. The question was reasonable enough. Why had we come here? On what errand? After all, we had not hired the car of our own accord. We had not settled the fare with the driver nor had we told him about our destination. We had not willed these things to happen. We had suddenly found ourselves in a car driven by a man who looked young but whose hair and beard were completely white. I thought, perhaps we have come to meet Babuji and to see his shop; how energetically he prepares himself every morning for work; how Ma sees him off at the front door; how he sells things at the shop throughout the day and comes back at night with the day's earning in a bag. Suddenly

I remembered how once, while he was returning home, a wayside filcher had snatched his bag from him. There was a total of sixty rupees in it. I am approaching sixty.

'Daddy,' my son says, 'where we live, there are five-star hotels. There are neither Hindu dharamshalas nor Muslim musafir-khanas. Where have you brought us?'

I exchanged a stealthy glance with my wife, avoiding the watchful eyes of our children. I wondered whether we are really like the heir to the shrine, dressed in black, looking at the dome in the graveyard of our past and when we feel shamed by the mean-inglessness of this whole exercise, we sit on our haunches with bowed heads. In the mausoleum, dervishes continue to chant *Ali da, Ali da*, swinging their heads from side to side.

In order to evade the question I said, 'Children, stay here for a while. We are going to find out why we have come here.'

We passed through a crisscross of broad and narrow roads and streets. When we got tired we stopped for a while.

'Should we call?' I asked my wife.

'Yes,' said my wife. 'Let's.'

We began to look for a place from where we could make a telephone call. After a long search we found a telephone in a butcher's shop. Slaughtered animals were hung all over. Blood glistened on their flesh. But the butcher was a perfect gentleman. At our request he allowed us to make the call.

Walking with some difficulty through the hanging carcasses my wife reached the telephone. She picked up the receiver and dialled a number. Wherever it was that she had called, someone answered and my wife said, 'Hello.' The person at the other end said, 'Wrong number' and the line got disconnected. My wife kept on trying but the result was the same. She got irritated and turning towards me said, 'wrong number! wrong number! What the hell! Whom are we ringing up, after all?'

'I don't know.'

She rushed out of the butcher's shop almost stumbling into the carcasses. The butcher warned politely, 'Take care, Begum Sahiba. Your clothes may get bloodstained.' My wife remembered she had not paid for the calls. She took out a ten-rupee note from her purse and held it out to the butcher, saying, 'Thank you very much, Bhai Sahab.'

The butcher gave a cursory glance at the tenner and then looked at us in surprise. 'I see! You have come from India.'

We were scared as though we had been caught stealing something.

'I beg your pardon,' he said, 'this currency is not in circulation here.'

I felt as if I had been struck by lightning. 'I see. This is at the crux of the matter. It is the currency which separates us and determines our nationality.'

My wife leapt to my side. 'This is terrible!' she hissed. 'We don't have a visa or a passport.'

I was scared stiff.

Lifting up my head I saw the butcher. He was regarding us as a policeman looks at a suspect.

'Listen,' I said, 'we stand to gain nothing by worrying. Only Anwar Sajjad or Intizar Hussain or Kishwar Nahid or Khalida Hussain can get us out of this mess.'

'Do you have their addresses and phone numbers?' my wife asked. 'No,' I replied and turned towards the butcher once again. He was a hefty, bespectacled man of middle age. I claimed his attention and said, 'Sir, we are in a fix. Do you know Anwar Sajjad?'

'Anwar Sajjad? Who's this Anwar Sajjad?' he asked in surprise.

'He runs a clinic in one of the cities.'

'Can you tell me the name of the city?'

'The name of the city . . . the name of the city . . .' I was muttering to myself, when a young man in a white shirt and trousers and a beautiful, black cap on his head came up to me and said respectfully, 'Salaam alaikum.'

'Walaikumsalaam.' I returned his greetings.

'I've come to receive you. Dr. Anwar Sajjad sent me.'

In a jiffy, the young man had put an end to all our difficulties. I felt like hugging him and kissing his forehead.

The next moment, a strange sight flashed before my eyes. He was my own son, standing before me in a different dress. But I asked myself, 'Why is he talking to me like a stranger?'

He said once again, 'Sir, my name is Abdus Salam. You can rely on me.'

The butcher said from the shop, 'Sir, this is my son.'

'Okay, let's go.'

We went along with him. After a few steps he stopped. One by one, several handsome young men, wearing similar bright dresses and elegant black fur caps, emerged and stood before us.

'Go on, move. Why don't you move?' my wife said impatiently.

'Sure, in a moment. It's just that we are waiting for the car,' one of the boys said respectfully.

And then, I was shocked to see that all the boys looked alike.

I said to my wife, 'We have no reason to worry now. We'll reach Anwar Sajjad's clinic by car. He'll let Intizar Hussain, Kishwar Nahid and Khalida Hussain know that we have arrived. You'll be delighted to meet Kishwar. She'll arrange to send you to Chakral, the home of your ancestors.'

'That's all right,' my wife said, 'but where have we left our children? They must be waiting for us.'

Suddenly, I realised my mistake. We had forgotten the road which would take us back to our children. Before us, there was a broad, transparent road on which bright new cars sped by. Around us were many children who all looked alike. How could we tell them that our children, too, looked the same as them and that we did not remember where we had left them?

My wife burst into tears.

Praise be to Allah that no one has come to hear of this sad story.

THE CURSE

MADHURANTAKAM RAJARAM

nominated by Vakati Panduranga Rao
translated by R. S. Sudarshanam

Have you ever been to Thondamandalam? It is certainly not a holy place like Kashi, Gaya, Kanchi or Rameswaram, worthy of a visit. Even if it were so, there's no rule that says one must go there.

There are about a thousand houses in Thondamandalam. If one takes into account the visitors who come here to see friends and relatives or on business, the population may not exceed a few thousand. If one of these visitors stays overnight, and also happens to be awake till after midnight then, in the stone-melting stillness of 1.30 am, he will hear a prolonged hoot *oooo . . . . woooo gug gug . . . woooo* piercing his ears like Yama's death arrow, filling his heart with fear and sadness like a curse of the village goddess, muttered

'Amba Palaku, Jagadamba Palaku' ('The Curse') was first published in Telugu in *Andhra Jyoti Illustrated Weekly*, April 5, 1990.

with a gnashing of teeth.

What bird is that? Whose is that accursed fate? Listen, for thereby hangs a tale.

It was twenty-five years ago. The time was just after midnight. The second film show at the theatre across the railway track had just broken for the intermission. The railway platform was full of passengers waiting for the late-running train from the west. The streetlights were burning dim because of the low voltage. The marketplace in the heart of the town was still active with people selling flowers and fruits, paan-bidi and soda.

Quite unconnected with the buzz of town life, at one end of the railway platform, some stray beggars and a few poor families had gathered together in a dilapidated goods-shed behind the East Cabin. Among them were two Sugali* couples, who made their living by hawking beads, hair pins, talcum powder and other such knick-knacks. The younger woman was busy cooking a meal while her husband smoked a leisurely bidi. The older couple was preparing to retire for the night after having eaten a supper made out of whatever was left over from their lunch. And, surrounded by their numerous children, the women of the bird-catcher's tribe were busy cooking hot and spicy dishes with the meat of squirrels and wild creatures caught by their menfolk during the day.

The cynosure of that little world of the dispossessed was an old bairagi seated in the centre of the shed in padmasana. He had silver hair and a flowing white beard. A tambura lay on his lap; he plucked at it with a single finger playing a single note in a steady rhythm. His eyes were closed but his lips moved, his song barely audible to the others.

The pot boiled over; the rice was cooked. The Sugali children got

Also known as Banjaras, the members of the Sugali tribe live in different parts of Andhra Pradesh, particularly, Rayalaseema and Telengana.

ready with their plates, eager for food. The beggars had come back from town and now lay all over the place, on stone benches and under the trees, for their night's sleep. The long-awaited train steamed into the station. Then the steps of the goods-shed resounded with the *kir kir* sound made by the old shoes of a visitor.

The Bairagi opened his eyes.

The visitor was in his fifties. He was lean and tall, and a little bent at the shoulders, like a bow. He wore a turban which was too large for his head. Thick eyebrows, a long moustache, and a month's growth of beard covered his face. A large dot of kumkuma in the centre of his forehead and small eyes sparkling like glow-worms attracted attention. He wore his dhoti wound tight round his legs like an armour, with the two ends tucked up firmly at the waist. His shirt was old and quite threadbare but it was well-concealed by his black coat. On his wrist he wore a metal charm and round his neck hung a string of black beads. Under his left arm was an umbrella and on his shoulder was slung a cloth-bundle which served as a bag. When he walked in, the goods-shed seemed to suddenly come alive, as if it were a theatre stage.

The Bairagi welcomed the stranger. 'Come, my son, sit here. Where do you come from?'

'My respects to you, Swami, my humble respects.' After a bow, the visitor laid his cloth-bundle on the floor, placed his umbrella on it, and with a shishya's devotion and respect, sat down before the Bairagi. 'I belong to a place near Koilkuntla in Kurnool district. My village is called Brahmagundam. We are a hundred houses. We stay in the village only for three months in a year. The rest of the time, for nine months, we travel around the country. We have faith in Lord Rama and we live by our faith. Swami, we are called the Budabukkalas*. My name is Mallanna. Budabukkala Mallanna.'

Budabukkalas are a nomadic tribe. They are Shaivites, worshippers of the consort of Shiva known as Kamakshi in Kanchi, Meenakshi in Madurai and Visalakshi in Kasi. The tribe derives its name from the *budabukka*, a small drum like that of Lord Nataraja.

'Is that so, my son! When did you arrive in this town?'

'This morning. I made a round of the whole town as soon as I got here. You know our professional routine, Swami. We start our rounds in the early hours of the morning. We need to find out in advance where the rich live, and where the poor, where the zamindars are located, where the farmers and where the business people. We have to find the right places where we may get a measure of rice, a quarter-rupee, an old shirt . . . for that is our living.'

'Well, my son, you seem to have surveyed the town. What is your impression?'

'There's an uptown and there's a downtown, Swami. The downtown is full of narrow lanes and small houses, like the rat-holes found in the fields. The poor and the daily-wage labourers who are to be found there, live from hand to mouth.

The middle section of the town consists of the bazaar — a very big one. In front you have the shops, and somewhere in the back are the residential quarters. One cannot hope for charity there, until the day has advanced and the shops have opened. In the south, the Kapus* have their quarters. They are middle-class people. They may say No but they invariably give away something or the other.

'Finally, in the north of the town, there is a large two-storied bungalow with a wall on all four sides. It is called Gundappa Mahadi. I understand that Gundappa died long ago, but there are three or four of his sons living, who own large properties not only there but also in the city. Inside that compound I saw cattle, tractors, workers, motor cars, scooters . . . the sight is beyond description. It is a veritable Vaikuntham, the abode of Lord Vishnu. The women there are fairer than goddesses, and the children sheer idols of gold. It is not samsara, but a ksheera-sagara on earth. One needs a thousand eyes to take it all in. If even one great man from that Mahadi

---

The Kapus who are Shudra by caste are an agricultural community.

chose to give charity, I'll be rich by a month's earnings.'

The Bairagi pursed his lips in dissent. The wrinkles on his forehead and the expression in his eyes indicated that he was struggling to tell the visitor an unpleasant truth. Finally he spoke. 'Mallanna, my son, I'll speak a word of advice. Would you care to listen?'

'Please do, Swami.'

'You go to the Kapu-quarters. They may give you little, but take it gladly. Visit the bazaar. If your luck is good, you may get ten or even twenty rupees. Put it in your pocket. Even downtown you may gather a few paise, for which you may feel grateful. But under no circumstance approach Gundappa Mahadi. Please do not go there.'

Mallanna looked doubtfully at the Bairagi. 'What is this, Swami? What do you mean, kindly explain.'

'Well, it is as I have said, my son! Some people don't show charity even to a poor cat. Some are not moved even if you cut your finger and bleed before them. And if you cut open your bowels to prove your honesty, they will only dismiss it as magic. Haven't you heard of them? That's the sort of people who live there. All of them born of the same house have built walls around their homes so that they may not see or be seen by the world outside. That is the Mahadi compound.'

'Even then . . . ?'

'My son, they consider their equals as worms, their inferiors as trash under their feet. They cannot understand why without food, shelter or clothing, the poor, the bastards, exist at all. Anyway, the world enclosed within those walls is of one kind and the world outside is altogether a different one. It is better that we live in ours and they in theirs. Mallanna, I have given you my advice. Do as you please . . . .'

'Kindly listen to what I have to say, Swami. I was not born yesterday, nor have I opened my eyes to the world today. For the last thirty-five years I have been wandering all over the country from Alampur to Anantpur, from Kavali to Kalahasthi. I have seen all the towns and villages in our area. I have met bigwigs, several of them. Before a non-giving, stubborn person, I am a persistent, immovable sticker . . . .' As he spoke these words, Mallanna was about to touch his moustache in a gesture of pride, but he desisted out of deference to the Bairagi's august presence.

The Bairagi was still patient. He gently resumed, 'Well, my son, I don't deny you have seen the world. A farm labourer is absent from work for two days on account of illness and he's tied to a tree and given a severe thrashing till he bleeds all over. Have you seen farmers punishing workers like that? A passerby gathers some fruits from their orchard — as a punishment, his head is shaved, and with the fruit-garland hung round his neck, he is paraded through ten villages in the neighbourhood. Have you ever seen farmers meting out such punishment? Because the sheep fail to fertilise the field in time, the poor animals are made to lie in the slushy field, and when they die, the man who ordered it twirls his moustache in glee. He summons the primary school teacher, who had the temerity to pull up his son in school, and orders him to keep standing for one whole day from morning to evening! Have you ever come across any farmer like him?

'You say that their women are fairer than goddesses. They are locked up in the houses and their beauty scorned while their lords take their pleasure with the bazaar-women. If these men were to stand for election, even their wives would not vote for them! Therefore, Mallanna, don't put your fingers in the fire, they are sure to get burnt. If you still say you don't mind, then I have nothing more to say.'

His head bent meditatively, Mallanna sat silent for a while, and then he stood up slowly. He took out from his cloth-bundle a gunny-sheet, made his bed and stretched himself. After a while, he opened his eyes and looked meaningfully at the Bairagi.

'Yes?' said the Bairagi.

'May I say a word and hope you will not take offence? Without touching fire, I think I can light my bidi.'

The Bairagi laughed and said, 'Well, well, my son.'

> *Speak Mother, Speak, O Mother of Universe!*
> *O Kamakshi in Kanchi, speak!*
> *O Meenakshi in Madurai, speak!*
> *O Mother who lives in Kadipuri,*
> *O Visalakshi, speak!*
> *Speak the truth,*
> *Speak of good tidings,*
> *Speak Mother!*

The darkness of night was dissolving and the air was cool with dew. The trees stood still. In the Mahadi, excepting for the main gate of the compound and the front door of the building, all the windows and doors remained closed. A middle-aged woman was sprinkling water on the ground in front of the house. When she saw Mallanna crossing the main gate, she came running towards him, gesturing at him to keep away.

'O budabukkala, how can you dare! Stop it, stop that noise right away and keep your peace. The master is asleep! If he is disturbed, he will flay you alive. Get away. Get lost and don't be seen anywhere near this place.'

'Such warnings are common and I take them in my stride,' thought Mallanna. He went ahead and took his stand on the stairs leading to the house. He guessed that the master of the house would be asleep in the room next to the front door. He raised the pitch of his voice. Whenever he paused in his song, he filled the gap with the ringing sound of his budabukka:

> *May Mahalakshmi, the goddess of wealth, abide in the maharaja's domain*
> *May prosperity arrive in a palanquin to inhabit this house*
> *May everything touched turn into solid gold*
> *May your touch yield pearls in plenty*

May all your wishes be fulfilled
Speak the truth, Mother
Speak of good tidings
Speak, mother of the Universe, speak . . . .

'Who is there?' The voice was like a thunderbolt.

The servant trembled. There were drops of sweat on her forehead though the morning air was cool. She ran up to the door and said in a quivering voice, 'It is a budabukkala . . . .'

'What does he want?'

Mallanna went up a few steps and whispered to the servant, 'Old clothes, old clothes.'

She conveyed the words to her master.

'Let him wait.'

There was triumph in Mallanna's eyes. Pleased, he looked at the servant. Then came a terrible, deafening bark, and before he knew what it was, a black dog was on Mallanna. Its long salivating tongue protruding, and its sharp fangs fully bared, the dog that fell on him was no ordinary dog. The animal put its fore-paws on Mallanna's waist, and pulled off his wrapper.

'My god, this is the end,' he cried and jumped off the stairs.

The hunting dog went after him and caught him in one quick bound, its sharp teeth not sparing anything that was within reach. The cloth-bundle was torn up, bits of the cloth dangled from the dog's mouth. Mallanna's possessions were scattered on the ground. When he tried to retrieve them, his coat was torn to pieces. The dog's fangs pierced through the shirt and Mallanna's back was soon full of red marks. His turban and umbrella had disappeared. He ran for his life holding onto his slipping dhoti with both his hands.

Mallanna realised that he would not get back any of his things. He must at least save his life. He fled like a dry leaf tossed in a whirlwind. He was not aware of what clothing remained on his body, nor was he aware of the cuts and scratches made by the dog's sharp fangs. He was aware only of one thing, and that was death. Death was the cruel, ferocious dog pursuing him.

The dog jumped on him throwing him to the ground. He tried frantically to shake it off using his hands and legs as best as he could. Mallanna stumbled forward crying wildly in his helplessness. Finally he got to the foot of a tree and managed to clamber up even as the dog kept pulling at his dhoti and snapping at his legs. It was an almond tree, quite bereft of leaves, like the one used in the theatre for Arjuna's penance. It appeared as a saviour to Mallanna. He climbed higher, beyond the reach of the dog and perched himself on a branch. When at last he gathered a little strength and collected himself, he realised that he had no clothes on him except for a piece of his coat hanging round his neck. His shirt might as well have not been there. His body, criss-crossed with cuts and scratches, felt like one raw wound. His dhoti lay at the foot of the tree. The dog kept watch around the tree looking up at him every now and then.

An hour might have passed.

A man, perhaps a servant, came through the gate towards the house, saw Mallanna's plight and immediately guessed what had happened. For a while he stood amazed and shocked. Then he went inside the house and brought back the dog-chain. Silently he chained the dog. Leading it away, he looked at Mallanna and signalled with his eyes, 'You pitiful idiot, get away, get away.'

Times have changed. Nay, men have changed. Every man in Thondamandalam, everyone with a head on his shoulders, has developed a desire for education — education which widens one's perspective on life and society. Ideas and opinions about a man's conduct towards his fellow men have taken definite form. It's a code that cannot be violated even if the violator be Lord Shiva himself. The educated youth have also convinced the older generation about the dignity of man and his rights.

Gradually people began avoiding the Mahadi. The fields remained untilled. Vexed with the people of Thondamandalam, the residents of the Mahadi migrated to the city. They invested all their money in business. Even though they understood that the fields would not yield anything, they could not make a final break with the house, which had become unsaleable. And a house uninhabited is like a corpse. There was no one to keep it free from dust, vermin, cobwebs and decay. No whitewashing and no repairs. Moreover, there was a rumour that the house was haunted by the spirits of those who had died there prematurely, or had been murdered and lay buried mysteriously in the compound. As the rumour gained currency, the Mahadi itself became ghostlike.

This story of social transformation is not, however, the story you hear in Thondamandalam. The people there tell you of Budabuk-kala Mallanna and trace the decay of Gundappa Mahadi to him. The tailend of Mallanna's story remains to be narrated for the sake of completion. After all, a temple is not complete without its gopuram.

Mallanna climbed down slowly from his perch on the tree and felt as if he was half dead. His appearance was that of a mad man. He collected his dhoti and covered his nakedness with it. Some distance away, among the crotons, lay his budabukka. His spirit revived on seeing it. It was his life's blood. He did not mind the loss of his other possessions now that he had recovered the budabukka. He hurried out of the prohibited area. Taking the shortest route, he came to the outskirts of the town.

To the north of the town was a stream and on the other side of the stream lay the cremation ground. He drank to his fill the cool water and then crossed over. He stood there under a tree, and taking from the ground a fistful of ash, he flung it in the air in the direction of Gundappa Mahadi. The budabukka in Mallanna's hand danced rhythmically and sounded like Shiva's own drum in the burial ground:

> *O Mother Kamakshi, if your presence in Kanchi be true*
> *O Mother Meenakshi, if your presence in Madurai be true*
> *O powerful Visalakshi, if your presence in Kashi be true*
> *Then may Gundappa Mahadi turn into a derelict ruin*
> *With no lamps lit*
> *With wild plants crowding the floor*
> *The owl perched on its roof . . .*
> ***Speak** Mother, Speak, O Mother of the Universe!*

HANDS

REKHA

nominated by Rajendra Yadav
translated by Ruth Vanita

T his is the last bus. Whatever happens, Saryu must catch this
bus. Suppose she were to miss it . . . .

She has let Salil know when she will arrive. He will wait for her
in the early morning light, leaning against that round pillar of cold
black cement. Missing this bus will mean a tedious daylong journey
tomorrow; Salil's disappointment, her own at not being present on
his birthday, and then, Salil's long, angry silence.

No. This must not be. She begins to run faster. The bus has begun
to rumble into life.

Tomorrow morning she will see the sun leap over the old church
tower and into the sky on the very edge of Salil's city. And if she
were to miss this bus . . . all she will have is this self-engrossed room

'Haath' ('Hands') was first published in Hindi in *Hans*, February 1988.

in the YWCA . . . the distorting glass of the windowpane, the crippled sun splintering through it.

But two more steps to go. The bus has started to move. She is thrust forward by the helpless shriek which is forced out of her. A hand emerges from the open door of the bus and pulls her in. A hand from amidst the crowd outside the bus pushes her in.

She is inside.

She had no choice. If she did not get to Salil's city by morning, it was possible that Salil and his city would be left behind forever. Saryu thanked her stars and sat down on the first empty seat she could find. She was still breathless. The little creature that lies quietly between the ribs had suddenly woken up and had begun to protest. It took her some minutes to calm it down.

It is dark inside the night bus. Not a black darkness but a deep grey darkness — drops of white moonlight have lightened the dense ink. Saryu could not see clearly or hear distinctly, but she was hit by a smell that told her that the bus was packed. The crowd swirled around her, but it was as if she was not in it. She was alone, unable to dissolve in the darkness. There were shadows melting into the darkness on either side of her. She began to see herself as a shadow.

. . . In the moment's pause before the mirror as she was leaving her room, she had looked at herself, enchanted. Her body was like a wave. A pearl-white sari. A long loose plait. Her hair falling over her ears like the gathering twilight. A white rose like the evening star. She smiled softly at herself. Then, seeing herself through Salil's eyes, she had murmured as he would, 'How dazzling . . . tell me Saryu, is this flower real or artificial?'

Suddenly, a smell of trickling sweat drifted into Saryu's nostrils. She took out a bottle from her bag, turned open the key-shaped lid, and put the bottle to her nose. She wanted to soothe her senses tortured by the odour of sweat; she had failed in her attempt to drink in the orange-flavoured fragrance of talcum powder rising from her breasts.

There came another wave of the same smell from somewhere. How oppressive it was. Saryu felt as if she were standing in a closed room with a heap of rotting vegetables, decayed fruits. Fungus-covered walls and piles of wet bread. A wave of nausea rose within her and she almost wept. Who are these people? For the first time, she was assaulted by the reality of their existence.

Something shone behind her. Like a cat's eye in the dark. A match. She shuddered as if the match had been struck on her back.

'Here, will you have a bidi?'

'Put it in my mouth with your own hands. I haven't been able to do it for a month now.'

'What? Really?'

'Did you see that ad at the bus stand? I hear that there are many cures available these days.'

'You think that's true?'

'True? Nothing but big words. Tell me, is she able to cook?'

'Yes. So far. Perhaps for another year ....'

'Where's she now?'

'With her mother. She's pregnant.'

'Ugh!'

'Listen, the child's hands will be all right, won't they?'

'So they say ... but ....'

Saryu jerked her head away. She tuned into another channel.

'Welcome, my dusky darling. How was the journey? Did you have a good night? Have some hot coffee first — then we'll go home. I've parked the car right here. How well you know me! This white silk sari, this long plait ....'

This channel too was cut off. Perhaps the bus driver had suddenly braked.

Saryu took out a packet from her bag. Light brown soft pash-mina gloves. A birthday present for Salil. She ran her hands over them gently. A hand, strong, well-made, beautiful, reassured her from inside.

Suddenly the touch was shattered. She felt something hard

scraping the uncovered part of her back. A horrible, rough touch. She squirmed. She wanted to remain untouched in her freshness for Salil. The continuous friction gnawed away at her patience. A centipede was crawling down her back. Its fine legs would scrape away first the skin, then the flesh and then, bone.

'No. No.' She turned round and pounced on the hand. But . . . what was this? She was stunned into immobility. Where was the hand? Only a palm. Knotted knobs in place of fingers. Like knobs of ginger. Wounded and injured.

Was this then . . . ? It was hard to read anything in the eyes that were raised towards her. Hardly eyes. Two deep oozing wounds. Wounds that could see.

Saryu understood. It was not the fulfillment of an unsatisfied desire that made the stump touch a living body; it was only an effort to feel itself alive. The fingers had dropped off like yellow leaves, but the desire to touch still oozed from their roots.

Suddenly, the paintings on the walls of the old church in Salil's city came to her mind. Unfortunate invalids ecstatic at Jesus' touch. In a flash that picture too disappeared into the darkness of the bus. The hand was once again outlined in its full deformity in the glow of the smouldering bidi.

Nausea welled up inside her. A fistful of ashes filled her mouth. She got up from the seat, wrapped her sari around her and moved further ahead.

She gazed into the darkness outside the window. It was perilous to catch another eye. The wound-like eyes were still on her back. Outside was a forest that had shed its leaves. Naked stumps . . . bare boughs outlined as in a picture. Leaves that went up flying as the bus sped on and then fluttered down to settle on the road once again. The stumps would green, again and again, but these withered hands?

'No . . .'

Once again, Saryu jerked her slender neck. The darkness of the bus was shattered by the light of a huge truck that came towards

them. The American diamond in her long thin nose sparkled for a
moment.

You are fast asleep now, Salil, while I cross the Vaitarini to reach
you. I would rather not have come by this bus, but what choice did
I have? On one side of the darkness the bus and you on the other.
How could I have known what was inside the bus? It was like fate
. . . unknown . . . dark.

What was this? The centipede was walking on her neck. She
moved and it fell to her waist. Hiding her hands in her sari, she
looked to the right. Her eyes stayed there. Another stump. A clumsy
hammer-like fist. Two dark holes in place of a nose. She felt as if in
a moment two lizards would peer out of them. A disintegrated face
and the oozing eyes. This was the man whose stump searched into
her soft skin for its lost sensations. She jumped up from her seat as
if she had stepped on a scorpion. She was thrown off-balance into
the seat in front of her. Two stumps, like a pair of tongs, emerged
from a torn kurta and helplessly tried to lift and support her.

She got up and staggered forward. She stepped on someone's
feet. He cried aloud and turned his face reproachfully towards her.
That face . . . whose face was it? Saryu turned white with fear.
Before her were the same speaking wounds, a dark cavernous nose,
salivating blue lips. Saryu felt that a demon was pursuing her, the
flames from his nostrils flaying her back.

A shriek was wrung out from her innermost self. She tried to
raise her hand to stop it. But breaking all barriers, it pounded the
silence of the forest.

Almost in a trance, Saryu muttered, 'my hands . . . where are my
hands? Two stumps, the paws of a thorny cactus . . . oozing wounds
in place of fingers . . . .'

The bus stops. Once again the invisible hands push her out.
Saryu wants to lift the palla of her sari, to touch the flower in her
hair, to touch her eyelashes. Are her eyes still beautiful today? She
wants to run her hand over her back . . . is the centipede still there?
Will Salil recognise her . . . will he?

Salil is coming towards her. Where are his hands? Why can't she see them? Are they in his coat pockets? Why in the pockets? Is this really his voice?

'Saryu, Saryu, are you here? What have you got hidden in your hands? See what I have for you in my hands. Have you gone dumb? Saryu?'

Salil grabs her hand and pulls it out from her sari. A fearful shriek is torn out of Saryu's throat. It flies out like a bird whose wings have been grazed by a stone . . . .

'Salil . . . your hands . . . you have hands . . . you really have. . . They are very beautiful . . . .'

NOMBU

FAKIR MUHAMMED KATPADI

nominated and translated by
K. Raghavendra Rao

Amma would fill each leaf with tobacco, fold it, make a mark with her fingernail, and then pass it on to her son. It was Addu's job to tie it with red thread and put it in the basket. Bits of scissored leaves stuck to Amma's sari, or lay scattered on the floor. Bidis lay heaped in the basket. The strong scent of tobacco dominated the air. The whole process was going on so smoothly, so silently, that from a distance it appeared as if the work was being performed by machine-like humans.

Amma would cough. Once in a while she'd stretch, draw her legs closer to each other, or shift her weight from one leg to the other. When the continuous squatting gave her a pain in her waist, she

'*Nombu*' (title of the original story) was first published in Kannada in *Sannekatha*, Karnataka Sahitya Akademi, 1987.

straightened her back and then lowered it. Maybe to forget the boredom, the physical drudgery, she would break into a traditional folk song like Moplah Patt or Maale. Whenever he found a familiar line Addu joined in, softly.

Suddenly the sound of a whistle assailed Addu's ears. Addu jumped. He peered out through the thatched door that had been left open to let some fresh breeze in. The whistles spilled into the hut, one after another.

Of course, Amma knew only too well that once he heard his friends at play, it would be impossible to keep her seven-year-old son indoors. Laughing inwardly, she said, 'At least finish the work on the leaves already snipped, child. Then you can go . . . though, nothing has been done yet about the fasting.'

Addu nodded reluctantly but, 'Amma,' he urged her, 'Amma, please! Pass the folded bidis faster.'

His mother smiled. 'Son, why such a hurry? If the bidis stick together, you know that the supervisor would crumple them and fling them away. How shall we feed ourselves then?'

They didn't notice Addu's father come in. He took off his shirt, hung it on the peg, spread the mat, then sat down, leaning against the pillar. Stretching his legs for comfort, Appa began to fan himself with his large handkerchief.

Amma saw him and her work slowed down.

The whistling outside seemed to intensify. Addu began to mutter, 'Amma, faster . . . .'

Appa sighed. 'Ya Allah! What heat! This time the nombu is going to be very tough. This sultriness, this heat . . . . I could not even lift four bags of tobacco . . . My eyes became blinded. And I still have twenty days of fasting. How am I going to manage?'

Amma looked as if she suffered each one of his pains.

'The morning's rice kanji is still there. Addu didn't eat much today . . . .' she said, a trace of doubt and reluctance in her voice.

'Che, che! Should one give up fasting for fear of such difficulties. May Allah forgive me. I must ready myself to endure the sun's heat

on the day of judgement at the Akhirat in the Mashara congrega-
tion. May we face all our trials in this life itself! Tomorrow after
death, at least in the Akhirat, may Allah grant us health and
prosperity.'

Amma's hands slowed down further. Addu began to grumble:
His friends would never let him join them if he kept on delaying
like this.

Amma turned on him angrily. 'Always grumbling,' she said.
'You have no patience whatsoever. All you can think of is play, play,
play . . . .'

'Oh, is that why he is creating all this fuss?' asked Appa. 'If he
wants to play, let him. Give me a few minutes, I'll help you tie up
the bidis.'

Addu jumped up. Not waiting for Amma's permission, he
scrammed to join his playmates.

The boys had staked out the vacant spot in the middle of the
coconut grove as their playground. They had a game to suit the
ground—Lagori. They would heap some eight to ten pieces of tiles,
and then from a distance of four to six yards they would aim a ball
at the heap. One team had to pick up the tiles and re-heap them
while their opponents hit them with the ball to get them out.
Apparently Sulaiman, the owner of the garden, hadn't heard the
boys at play. After the Lohar Namaaz he might have gone to sleep
or even gone to the town market. Otherwise, surely he'd have
chased them away. 'Shaitans!' he would have screamed. 'You've
killed all my coconut plants. Because of the evil deeds of you devils,
the platforms round my coconut trees have been ruined . . . ' But
this was the only suitable spot for play and the boys used every
trick they could to avoid Sulaiman.

When Addu reached the playground, he went straight up to
Sharif. 'Please take me in your side,' he begged.

Sharif turned to Zuber. 'If you want, you can have him.'

Zuber now ran his eyes over Addu's body. The frail, bony Addu struck him as a liability. The only thing that stood out was his bright face. His big shining eyes. Zuber announced his decision in one word: 'No.'

'You were late, Let's see after this game,' Sharif said. And all Addu could do was to go sit under a coconut tree, watching the others at play and praying that Sulaiman Saab would come and puncture their arrogance. Kashim who came even later than Addu also had no chance to play. The two boys sat staring at each other. The game was in full swing.

'Are you fasting during Ramzan, Addu?'

'No. My mother says children don't have to.'

'Yes, that is what my mother also says. I want to ask her today to allow me to take part in Attaya at least. Do you know the story of a boy who did fasting? My mother tells it. It is a beautiful story. Addu, would you like to visit our house?'

Addu was bored sitting there. 'Yes!' he said, promptly.

Kashim's backyard started where Sulaiman Saab's garden ended. And as they walked there, Addu asked, 'Kashim, do you know anything about this nombu?' Addu knew that nombu meant not eating any food from morning to sunset. But he had never fasted.

'I don't know,' Kashim confessed. 'When I ask Amma, she says I'm too young and that when I grow up I'll get to know. She says the Quran Mushaab came down to earth in the month of Ramzan. She says the doors of heaven are open throughout this month. It seems all those who fast during Ramzan will enter heaven. That is what Amma says.'

'Kashim, isn't heaven something we can get only after we die? I wish we could get it *now* itself!'

They say it's first class there! There are beautiful houries like Hoorullin. You remember what the Moulvi told us? He said that what is evil on this earth becomes good in heaven.'

There was a hint of sarcasm in Kashim's tone.

As if to match his friend's knowledge, Addu said, 'Yes, there's happiness and prosperity there. Bellyfuls of food. Plenty of oranges, apples, and grapes. Cooked meat and ghee-rice every day. There will be lots and lots of neatly-pressed striped silk shirts, silk lungis and velvet caps with golden embroidery!'

Kashim laughed. 'You don't need to go to heaven for these things. We already have them in our house.'

Then Kashim's house must be a heaven, Addu thought. He started walking faster.

Kashim's house was large and wonderful. The floor shone as if freshly washed. There were chandeliers burning white. The walls were painted in bright colours. There were soft cushioned seats. The window curtains had beautiful flowers on it. Kashim's father was sleeping on a soft bed in a beautifully decorated room. Addu was impressed. Heaven must be like this, he thought. Kashim's mother was making akkirotis in the kitchen. As he entered it, Addu shrank into himself.

'Back so soon, Kashim? Would you like some akkirotis?'

'Amma, Addu has come with me. Will you give him akkirotis, too?' Kasim asked, pointing at Addu.

'Oh, it's beedi-Khader's son . . . . You can both eat together.'

Addu washed his hand with water shooting from a tap. Then he sat down before the plate.

The akkiroti was paper-thin and smeared with ghee. The mutton curry was delicious. It was the meal that the family ate together in the evening to end the Ramzan fast. Addu's mother made crude, thick akkirotis. Once he had asked her to make thin ones and she'd said, Where do I have the time to indulge in such nonsense Addu? I have to get back to the bidis. Addu decided that he must ask his mother to cook thin akkirotis that day.

'Amma,' Kasim was asking, 'you too keep the fast but you don't sleep in the day. Why?'

His mother laughed. 'Who is to do the household chores and

cook the food that breaks the fast? My dear child, can a woman afford to feel tired like men and indulge in sleep?'

Kashim's elder sister Jameela walked into the kitchen. 'Arey! The sun has not yet set, and you have already started to break the fast!' she teased.

'I don't observe the fast, Jameelakka ....'

'Don't you know that those who don't fast should not eat openly like this?'

Amma looked up. 'Why do you harass them, Jameela? Now you wash the rice and start cooking it ... children, finish eating.'

Addu gave a sigh of relief when Amma sent her upstairs, saying, 'Jameela, go find out if your husband is awake and needs something...'

'Brother-in-law has come,' Kashim whispered in Addu's ear, 'This is my brother-in-law's first nombu after the marriage and this evening we are going to celebrate when he breaks it. Amma has made mutton samosa, semia payasam, and all sorts of delicious things.'

Addu wanted to take part in the celebration. 'How does your brother-in-law break his fast, Kashim?'

'This is how,' said Kashim. 'First they spread a carpet. Then they spread a beautiful cloth over it. They put coloured chinaware filled with sherbat, firni, samosa, payasam, badam, dates, oranges, apples, and grapes. After the sun sets, brother-in-law and all of us sit around it, say Bismilla, and then we all eat. Do you know that in our grandfather's house even now my Appa is invited to the nombu feast?'

Addu imagined the festivities in great detail. Allah has given Kashim's people a heaven on earth, he thought. Though Appa says that we shall go to heaven after death, I wish Allah had given us also a bit of heaven here itself!

Jameela came back. 'He is still asleep,' she said, starting to knead the dough with her mother.

'Amma, will you tell us the story of the fasting boy? Addu has come to hear you.'

'Tell Addu the story I told you yesterday. I have no time!'

'No, I don't know how to tell a story. You tell him, Amma. You tell it so beautifully!'

Addu leaned forward eagerly.

'Should one tell the story of the fasting boy to those who do not observe fasting?' Jameelakka asked, grinning. She looked a little pale, maybe because of the fasting. Her lips looked white. But Addu thought she looked very pretty because of her dimples. He wished he had a sister like Jameelakka.

'When you turn so stubborn, Kashim, I never manage to get anything done. Your teacher should not close the madrasa during the fasting period,' said Kashim's mother. 'Well, listen! In a town, there was once a seven-year-old boy. Like you.'

As she told the story, her hands continued to make akkirotis. The boy in the story was stubborn. He stuck to his decision to observe the fast in spite of his mother's opposition. His face wilted, his body dried up and, by the evening he was dead. Then, a messenger of Allah came in the guise of a fakir and brought the boy back to life with Allah's mercy. The tale ended with the boy living happily thereafter with his parents.

Addu was thrilled by the story. Kashim's mother had a beautiful way of telling it. He couldn't wait to get home to ask his mother if she knew the story. And he decided immediately that he'd somehow make his mother let him fast the next day. He was confident that if he were to die, Allah's messenger would come and save him. He knew that Allah granted all prayers when the devotee was fasting and he wanted Allah not to give any hardships to his Appa and Amma. He would beg Allah to grant them a palace like the one Kashim's parents had, and lovely clothes and . . . .

Addu finished eating the akkirotis and washed his hands. 'Shall I go home now?' he asked Kashim.

Still under the spell of the tale, Kashim just nodded. But, Kashim's mother said, 'Tell your mother to visit us during the days of the festival. We shall give her the remainder of this season's alms of rice and money.'

Addu mumbled a 'yes' and ran out. As he reached the outer courtyard, he saw the steps to the first floor. Curious to see Kashim's brother-in-law, he quickly climbed the steps.

The door of the room was slightly ajar. Addu pushed it gently open. A man was lying on a beautiful, thick, pink mattress. As Addu peeped in, he sat up. 'Who are you, boy?' he asked.

'I am Addu . . .'

'Come here.'

Addu stepped gingerly into the room. Over his head wheeled a fan, cooling the room. From its centre hung a golden chandelier. There were pretty window curtains. The room was strewn with bottles of scent specially sold during the festival. The smell was overwhelming. Addu felt that Kashim's brother-in-law was fortunate to live in that heaven. Jameelakka was the houri Hurunnisa from heaven.

'Can you get me a packet of cigarettes? But don't tell anyone.' Jameelakka's husband gave Addu a ten-rupee note.

Addu said, 'But the fast?'

Kashim's brother-in-law laughed.

Once in the street, Addu transformed himself into a bus . . . rrr . . . rrr . . . He ran to a halt just before Soorappa's paan-bidi shack. Stretching out his palm with the ten-rupee note in it, Addu said, 'A packet of cigarettes . . .'

When he was returning, he bumped into the priest Ismail Haaji.

'And for whom are these cigarettes, pray, in these days of fasting?' Ismail Haaji asked.

Addu mumbled.

'Must be for your Appa!' The priest's lips twisted in anger. 'Such thinking has brought evil to us. You people don't become barquat because you don't practise Islam.'

Addu felt so angry to hear this unjust accusation, but he thought he'd keep quiet for the sake of Kashim's brother-in-law. Appa and

Amma always fast and say the namaaz, and yet we never become barquat. Suddenly he heard himself say, 'It is not for Appa.'

Haaji said stiffly, 'You don't need any training in lying. You are after all your father's son . . . . '

Addu felt like weeping. He turned and fled.

As he climbed the steps in Kashim's house, he heard voices. Kashim's brother-in-law was saying, 'Do as I say! If you utter one word in opposition I shall smash your thigh . . . ' and Jameelakka replied, 'How much money do you want me to squeeze out of Appa? How can we manage if you don't earn anything? How much more can Appa shell out?'

Addu heard the sound of a sharp blow.

He would have run away except for the cigarette packet and the change in his hands. He knocked. After a brief pause, Kashim's brother-in-law opened the door. Jameelakka wiped her tears and left the room.

Addu was about to leave the place, when he saw the man put the cigarette between his lips and light it. He blurted out, 'If you smoke a cigarette, your fasting will lose its value.'

'You dare teach me what I should do . . . . '

As Addu took the steps two at a time, he remembered the words, 'There is no evil in heaven. What is evil on earth also becomes good in heaven!'

Then, wasn't Kashim's house heaven?

Addu reached the courtyard to find Kashim's father shouting at a beggar who always stood in front of the mosque. He was known to be mad. 'Don't you know this is a day of fast? You are asking us to feed you, aren't you ashamed of yourself? That is why Allah has made you into this. Now be off.'

The beggar laughed in a peculiar way and then walked away. Addu knew that this man went only to Muslim houses. He grinned. 'Even this mad fellow must fast for a day . . . . '

Kashim's father turned towards Addu. He was still angry. 'Why are you standing here, boy? Go home!'

Addu had not expected this. Scared and tearful he found himself running away as fast as he could.

Back home, Addu found Appa folding the bidis as well as tying them. Amma was inside, cooking the evening meal. She was coughing now and then. Appa, too, was coughing occasionally.

Addu ran straight to his mother. 'Amma I want to fast tomorrow,' he said eagerly.

'Child, listen. It is not compulsory for you. Don't do it.'

But Addu kept insisting till his mother gave in. When Addu skipped out of the kitchen, Appa asked him, 'Oh? So my son is fasting tomorrow?'

'Yes,' said Addu, proudly. Then, 'Appa, Allah grants all prayers to someone who's fasting, doesn't he?'

Appa continued to make the bidis. 'What is it that my darling son will beg from Allah?' he asked.

Addu couldn't remember what he had wanted to ask Allah. Then he heard Appa cough again. His body moved so violently that bidis fell out of the basket. As he picked them up Addu said, 'Appa, I'll pray that your cough and Amma's should be cured . . . .'

A smile formed on Appa's face. For a moment he stopped his work, pulled Addu into a tight embrace. 'Child,' he said, 'this cough is glued to us for life. It will leave us only in our tomb.' He gave a deep sigh. 'Ya Allah, if only it were possible to release our son from it,' he muttered, lifting his half-closed eyes towards the heavens.

While Addu helped his Appa, he recalled the words of the priest during the Darsi: Allah is One. He has been there always. He is without beginning. He has no family and no family ties . . . .

Eyeless Allah saw everything. He would have watched Kashim's brother-in-law smoking the cigarette. He must have seen his Appa continue with the fasting in spite of his coughing and his giddiness, Addu said to himself, yet Kashim's brother-in-law is in a heavenly house and we are in a thatched hut. Why? May be after our death, Allah has planned to put us in His heaven, as Appa says. Then, suddenly remembering, he shouted, 'Amma, Kashim's mother said you must visit them during the festive days, and they will give you Zakhat money and rice.'

Amma sounded annoyed. 'Where is the need for us to stretch our hands for alms?'

In the evening Kashim came to Addu's hut. He said, 'Addu, today our people have taken snacks and fruits and sherbat to the mosque. Today's festivities will be at our expense. Will you also come?'

But when Addu asked her, his mother said, 'Only those observing nombu should go. If you eat there, you will be reducing the share of those who had fasted. No, son. You can accompany Appa to the Thravih namaaz.'

Addu repeated her words to Kashim. But maybe Kashim would like to come with Addu for the namaaz?

Kashim looked hurt but he agreed to come with Addu.

That night, Addu's mother coaxed him to wear a lungi, a shirt and a small cap. In grand style Addu followed his Appa to the mosque.

There were already a few children and elders when they reached the mosque. Addu melted into the group of children. Sharif, Zuber, Kareem, Hanif, Lateesh and Basheer were busy giving an account of their fasting. Addu pulled a long face when he saw Sharif and Zuber. Sharif said that he had completed twelve fasts. Addu interrupted him. 'He is bluffing! He has just finished ten . . . .' All the boys burst into laughter. Sharif looked uncomfortable, but Addu felt pleased with himself. He'd made up for his defeat on the playground that morning.

Uncle Abu's voice came booming to them. 'Shhh! Boys, boys! If you don't keep quiet, I shall order you out!'

A hush descended. As they saw the elders performing the namaaz, the children followed suit. By the time the elaborate and long Thravih namaaz was over, Addu was tired out.

It was midnight when father and son returned home. Addu who was to fast the next day was too excited to sleep well that night.

When the cock-crow announced the dawn and the Attaya Kotis went round, beating their drum and chanting, 'It is time to do the Sahari . . .' Addu jumped out of bed, briskly.

His mother was already busy in the kitchen. 'Why don't you sleep some more, son?' she asked.

But Addu wanted none of that! After washing up along with his father, he sat down to a meal of smoked dry fish, and chutney. Then, Appa taught Addu the Niyyat. It ran, '*Navait Soumukhdin an aadai pharal raaamlani haadihissanathi Allahi thiala. . .*' meaning, 'I am determined to undertake for Allah's sake tomorrow's fast as this year's obligatory act during the month of Ramzan.' Addu repeated after his father till the Subah Bhaang rang out from the mosque.

Appa went for namaaz, while Addu went back to sleep.

By the time he got up, the sun was already quite high. Addu sat up feeling wonderful that he was fasting. He wanted to wash his face and immediately go tell Kashim the news. But, as he reached Kashim's house, he stopped. Suppose he were to see Kashim's father first? He waited in the shade of the coconut tree in front of the house, waiting for someone to come out.

After a while, he saw Jameelakka. 'Oh, it is the boy who does not fast,' she said, laughing.

Her laughter sounded strained. Her face looked sad.

'I am fasting today,' Addu declared.

'Is that so?' she asked then fell silent.

'Is Kashim observing the fast?'

Addu had to repeat the question before she answered. 'Yes,' she said. 'But his fasting is only during certain intervals. Between the early morning snacks and the noon lunch; then between lunch and the evening snacks, and finally between that and the night meal! He does this daily. Is your fasting also of the same type?'

'No, mine is a genuine fast!'

Jameelakka's mind had wandered again.

'Where is Kashim?'

'Must have gone somewhere to play.'

Addu turned to leave when she called him back.

'Addu, will you do something for me?' she asked. 'But you must promise never to tell anyone. You have to swear to me.'

Addu nodded.

'You know the thembi tree by the riverside? I want you to get me two fruits from that tree. But promise first. You must never *ever* tell anyone about it!'

Addu knew this was not going to be easy. But it was Jameelakka. 'Okay, I'll get them,' he said. 'You stay here . . . .'

He climbed the tree, plucked two thembi fruits, and brought them to her. As she took them, her hands shook.

'What are these fruits for?' Addu asked

'To eat and die.'

'If you eat it, your fasting will be useless.'

She said nothing for a while. Then, 'Don't tell anyone about it,' she said. 'Now go and play. Go!'

Maybe Jameelakka, like her husband, wants to violate the rule of fasting secretly; perhaps she is not observing fast at all, Addu thought as he went off in search of Kashim.

He found Kashim near the topfruit tree.

'Aren't you fasting?' he asked Kashim.

'Yes! And you?'

'I am fasting too! Why are you picking those fruits — wouldn't it cancel your fasting?'

'It's not for eating now, Addu!' said Kashim patiently. 'I'll eat it at the time we break the fast, when it gets dark. Want some?'

Addu pocketed the fruits that Kashim gave him and then they went in search of other friends. But by the time Addu could spread the news of his fasting, it was past noon.

Kashim said, 'Wouldn't this fasting be better if we were allowed to drink a little water. What do you think?'

Addu felt like agreeing. That would be such a relief for Appa after a hard day's work. Kashim began to sing:

With the salt I ate
Water I drank
Allah, give me
The benefit of a fast.

Kashim somersaulted and jumped as he sang. It was a mad dance. Addu stood laughing. Suddenly Kashim stopped his antics. 'I must go home,' he said abruptly and left. Not knowing what to do alone, Addu too walked homeward.

No one was at home. Amma had bolted the door with a piece of rope and had gone to fetch water. Addu was sitting near the door, dozing, when she arrived carrying the pots. As she opened the door, she said, 'My child, the fast must have made you tired. You shouldn't have gone about in the sun. Go, go inside, spread the mat and sleep on it.' She ran her hand over his head. 'How is the fast going? Would you like to eat?'

'No, I shall not give up the fast!' Addu said, seeing before his mind's eyes the face of the fasting boy.

'All right. But do not run about in the sun any more. Sleep.'

As his mother put the pots on the floor. Addu moved close to her wondering if he should ask her something.

Amma seemed to sense this. 'What is it?' she asked.

Addu remembered he had sworn on Jameelakka's head that he'd keep her secret. 'Nothing, Amma,' he said. But curiosity overcame the desire to keep the oath, and Addu asked, 'Amma, wouldn't a fast lose its value if one ate thembi fruit?'

Amma turned pale. 'Who ate the fruit? It is poisonous!'

Addu shivered in great fear. 'That Kashim's sister . . . Jameelakka, Amma. She only asked me to bring her the fruits . . . I picked them from the tree by the riverside.'

How was Addu to know that the fruits were poisonous. He only knew that the dried fruits were used by the boys as balls. He only knew that when it was split open it contained some white pulp inside.

Amma looked really frightened. 'Why did you give them to her? People die when they eat it . . . .'

She quickly bolted the door and began to walk towards Kashim's house. Addu followed her. He said to himself, 'Ya Allah, let nothing happen to Jameelakka. I swear that I shall never again take her those fruits even if she demands them.'

They entered 'Jannat-ul-Firdous,' Kashim's house, and Addu's mother immediately called out to Jameelakka's mother. Breathless, she said, 'Where is Jameela? It seems our boy here gave her thembi fruits . . . .'

Kashim's mother immediately began to wail. 'What evil spirit has possessed her? Ya Rabbana . . . . At what evil moment did she marry the fellow? My girl is pure gold, and they consigned her to the custody of vultures greedy for money.' She rushed upstairs, Addu's mother following her.

Jameelakka was sleeping on the bed.

Running to her side, Kashim's mother said, 'Why did you do this, child . . . .' She touched her body.

Addu who had followed took hold of Kashim's hand and said, 'Your sister has eaten thembi fruits. My mother says that if anyone eats them they will die . . . '

Everybody was frightened at the way Jameela was lying. Her eyes were closed. When Addu's mother touched her and gently shook her, Jameela opened her eyes slowly. Perhaps the tears had been held back by the closed eyes, but now they began to stream down. Kashim's mother was sobbing again. 'Why are you tormenting me like this? If you had not been born in my belly, I would have said you were no child of mine, not born at all . . . You were born to kill me . . . .'

'Why did Akka want to die?' Addu asked his friend in a fierce whisper.

Kashim did not reply.

Addu grew suspicious. He ordered, 'Kashim, open your mouth, let me see!'

Kashim slowly opened his mouth. There was chocolate there.

'Your fasting is invalid!' Addu said triumphantly.

Kashim nodded his head like an accused.

Addu's mother was gently passing her hand over Jameela's head. She said, 'No matter where they are, women have the same fate . . . they have to endure everything . . . Allah has declared suicide to be a sin . . . .'

Addu and Kashim were set the task of scouring the room for the thembi fruits.

Jameela looked forlorn. 'I split them and ate them. Yet I did not die. I merely vomitted twice or thrice . . . That was all.' She gave a dry laugh. Her face looked bleached, the eyes sunken. Her lips were dry. Addu felt like crying when he saw her.

'It is better to consult a doctor . . . .' Addu's mother said.

Kashim's mother was wailing loudly.

Amma turned on Addu. 'It was all because of you. Just because she wanted them, why did you have to fetch them for her?' she asked. But, Kashim's mother hushed her. 'He is a mere child. What does he know? Halima, why do you take him to task like that?'

'The truth is that women should not be born on this earth . . . .' Amma said with a sigh then, turning to Jameela, 'Jameela, I have plenty of work to do. We have to live somehow till we die on this earth . . . .' Then, Amma took Addu's hand in hers, and left.

All the way home, Addu's head was filled with the question of why Jameelakka had tried to kill herself. He knew that after a person is buried, two of God's messengers called Mallaks enter the tomb, resurrect the body, and interrogate it. This is called Chothiya. They ask, What is your name? What is your Deen? Can you recite the Shahadat Kalma? What are the tasks of Islam? How many Eemaon tasks are there? and so on. In the madrasa the Moulvi had taught: Those who give the correct answers to these questions will go to heaven. Those who have committed evil deeds will not be able to move their tongues during the interrogation. Pray to Allah to grant us the company of those bound for heaven. Addu knew how to answer these questions correctly and promptly. All this had been taught to them by the Moulvi. But Addu also knew that the divine messengers were forbidden to ask these questions during Nombu. There would be no punishment for those who didn't know the answers. As Addu recalled all this, he thought that that was why Jameelakka had tried to die when she did.

'Amma,' he said, 'During the Ramzan month, the Kabar pond does not contain Chothiya. Perhaps Jameelakka wanted to die because during the Ramzan all the doors of heaven are open, and she can easily enter . . . .'

Amma could not help smiling. She said, 'Maybe,' and fell silent.

But then, why didn't she die in spite of her eating the poisonous fruits? Addu could not solve the puzzle of why people who possess heavenly houses even on this earth should be so anxious for the heaven of the Akhirat.

Amma suddenly remembered something. 'Ayyo,' she said. 'How forgetful I have become. I had invited Aminamma, Jainaabi and others to say the Thauba today. Now it's already time for the Asar namaaz. Perhaps they are waiting in front of our house. Let's hurry.'

During Ramzan the women of their neighbourhood who could not read the Quran came to hear Addu's mother recite the Thauba. They fervently repeated the lines and begged Allah's forgiveness for their evil deeds and errors. From His inexhaustible treasury of compassion, He would grant them happiness and prosperity. He would open wide the gates of His heaven, the Jannat-ul-Firdous, and welcome the faithful.

As Amma had expected, women had gathered before the house. She was apologetic. 'You've been waiting for long. I shall finish my Asar namaaz quickly. Please be seated.'

She unfastened the rope and opened the door and went inside. The women trooped in and squatted.

'Addu!' Amma called him to her. 'Never say a word about Jameela to anybody. Why should we get entangled in other people's lives? We are poor folk, and they will not let us off easily if they find out that we've been talking about their family.'

Addu nodded his head. Amma went in to perform the namaaz. Addu squeezed himself into the room where the women were, next to a rolled mat.

'Do you observe the fast, child?' Aminamma asked.

'Yes!'

'A smart boy,' they said in chorus.

Jainaabi said, 'Your friend Zuber now. He eats three times a day, and never observes the fast.'

Addu remembered what Zuber had said in the mosque. 'He lied to me that he was observing the fast.'

The women laughed.

Addu muttered, 'It is a sin to lie.'

After finishing her namaaz, mother taught the women the Tauba. She began with the Arabic words, *Asthagfirullah-al-aleem*, and then translated it. The women repeated exactly what Addu's mother recited. Addu leaned against the rolled mat and went to sleep.

When he opened his eyes, Appa was already home. Saying, 'Our child is fasting today, I brought these things,' he handed over to Amma some cooling seeds and packets of wheat semia.

Addu was happy to hear of sherbat and payasam. He sat up.

'Our child is already awake . . . .' Appa said, running his fingers over Addu's head, when someone called from outside.

It was the mad beggar who had stood before Kashim's house. He made signs as if to say, 'Please give me something to eat.'

Appa said aloud, 'Poor man, he must be very hungry. Have you anything in the house?'

'The rice meant for Addu is there untouched,' Addu's mother answered from the kitchen 'You can give it him.'

Appa went and got the rice. The madman began to gobble it up.

It was evening. Addu remembered that in the story the boy had died at about this time, and then God's messenger had arrived in the guise of a beggar. Addu suspected that the mad beggar whom they had just fed, was perhaps that divine messenger. He approached the beggar who was busy eating. He asked him, 'Are you Allah's messenger?'

The mad man raised his head, stared at Addu, and began to laugh.

Addu felt disappointed. How can this fellow who does not fast be God's messenger? If Kashim's father were around, he would have shooed him away. Then why does Appa watching the mad fellow eat merely saying, 'Who knows how long he has been starving?'

The sun went down. From the mosque came the Bhaang of the Magrib namaaz. It was time to break the fast. Addu became thoughtful once again. He had not died like the boy in the story. No messenger of God had arrived.

Addu's parents sat by him when Addu completed his first fast by drinking the sherbat made of cooling seeds. Suddenly he remembered something, and fumbled in his pocket. He found the two topfruits given by Kashim. They tasted a bit sour and a bit sweet. They reminded him of Kashim. And the questions came back to him: How did the boy in the story die after one day's fasting? Why didn't I die?

Finding Addu silent, Amma asked, 'How did you find your fast, son?'

'Oh,' said Addu. 'Is this nombu? We have done this many times. Remember that day Appa was in the hospital and you made the bidis . . . No rice was cooked, and it was like this!'

Amma stared into Appa's face.

Appa said, 'Our son remembers everything.'

THE WHEEL OF FIRE

T. PADMANABHAN

nominated by Ayyappa Paniker
translated by Chandrika Balan

The bellowing of the cow was heard all night long. He could not get even a wink of sleep. Sometimes the cry sounded very near, at other times it seemed to come from far away. It was the cry of a mother cow separated from her calf, a cry of pain caused by udders weighted with milk.

He too was quite restless. More than once he left his bed to go over to the window and look outside. It was a moonlit night. The breeze that blew in was cool and comforting. The treetops glistened with dew. At any other time he would have stood there, quite lost in the silent music of nature. But today it was only the cow that mattered.

'*Kathunna Rathacakram*' ('The Wheel of Fire') was first published in Malayalam in *Kalakaumudi*, September 17-23, 1987.

Was it somewhere? Anywhere? Among the shrubs behind the house? Or in the wide open space beyond that? On the narrow pathway that runs for miles along the small canal? In the thick bamboo forests beyond the dam? Where could the cow be? His eyes and ears, and his mind went searching. He could not find the cow. As time passed he could hear the cry only intermittently. And then, it stopped completely.

He stood there, distraught.

From the bed his wife was watching him with impatience. She said, her voice hard, 'Come and lie down. It's only two o'clock.'

He hadn't realised that he was being watched. He hesitated for a moment, then, 'Please come here and look,' he said.

'It's night. Time to sleep.'

'Come,' he said again.

'That cow . . .' he murmured, when she finally came and stood beside him. 'I heard it all through the night. It seemed to come from very near. Then it stopped. Now it can't be heard at all.'

She did not say anything. After a brief silence, he asked her, 'Do you hear anything at all?'

'No.'

'I wonder where it went. And that little calf . . . without seeing its mother . . . .' He spoke like one who had lost something.

On any other day his wife would have found fault with him. She might have said, 'Ah, so you've lost your interest in cats and turned to cows.' Or, 'Cats, dogs, and now cows, what next?' Or, something sharp like that. But now, she merely said in a nicely-controlled voice, 'Come, come to bed.' And like a small child, he obeyed.

But he could not sleep. Neither could his wife.

'How many days is it since the cow's been lost? Three? Four?' she asked. 'It might have wandered off or someone might have taken it. How can it come back now? And supposing it does not come back. What is it to us, anyway? It's not our cow! Can't we get milk from someone else? Just because some woman has lost her cow, you . . . if people come to know how you've been fussing, won't they say you are mad?'

He had nothing to say to her but he thought: Will they think I'm mad? But that's what they think even now. At least some of the top officers do. And did you say *some woman*? Never! She can never be that. She has supplied us with milk for all these years. How can she suddenly become *some woman*? Never.

Memories of his mother gradually filled his mind, like light pushing open the door of darkness. And with her came all the cows that she used to look after . . . Yasoda, Nandini, Sharada . . . like her own children. She never sold them when their milk ran dry. She never sent them to the butcher when they became too old. Yet she was poor and had a tough time bringing up her own children. When people prodded her about her decisions, she said, How can I? Will I ever sell my children? They shall stay with me, eating a share of whatever is available. Nothing else is possible.

He remembered it all with some pain. The woman who had been providing them with milk all these years . . . . Wouldn't she have said the same?

At four o' clock in the morning he left the house for his walk. Usually he went along the road that ran around the neighbouring houses. Sometimes he chose the road that went to the city some miles away. But on mornings when the moon was still up, he liked to go over the dam and into the forest and be quite lost in the trees there. The past three mornings too he'd gone out into the wild countryside, but not to enjoy its beauty. Could the cow have gone there somehow? he wondered. It was not possible. But then, how could he be certain?

Gurkha Ram Singh was on duty at the gates of the dam. Recognising him from afar, he began, 'Saab, I was off-duty yesterday, so I went into the forest to look for it. No saab, there's no cow to be seen anywhere. I don't think it came this way. And you know saab, we'd never let it go in if it did come this way.'

Just as he had thought. Yet this is no extra work for me, no loss either. I come here on my usual rounds. And if I were to see the cow, just like that, suddenly?

If he asked them, Ram Singh or the other guards would not say no. They would find the cow, somehow or the other. They would be only too happy to oblige him. But his wife, she'd say, You're a top officer. Yet you go out of your way to look for a cow! Shame! If people come to know of it . . . . I don't understand!

I don't understand either, he thought.

Three days ago when he had gone into the kitchen, his wife had said, 'It's black tea today.'

'Why? What happened?'

She pulled a face. 'Well, what do you think has happened? There's always some excuse. This morning she came and said that her cow which had been let loose after the morning's milking, had not yet come back. And then she began to cry. What's the use of crying? And what about our milk?' When he stood silent, she said, 'Haven't I been telling you for ages that we should ask the dairy or someone else?'

He did not stay to hear more. He was in a hurry to leave for work. But on the way he remembered his mother all over again. She would wait anxiously at the door when a cow had not come back in the evening. And if it did not turn up at all, however dark it was, he and Amma would go in search with a chootu to light their way. They would walk over narrow paths, through fields and along the banks of the river, and whenever they thought they heard something stir they would call out 'Yasoda!' or 'Sharada!' Then when the cow was found. Amma would say, her voice at once full of love and reproach, 'Oh my daughter, you've caused us all so much worry.'

He was in the forest beyond the dam. The light of the setting moon fell around him through the bamboo growth like silver coins. Wild hares ran past, almost from between his feet. He thought he saw half-eaten grass fall off from their mouths. They ran for a bit, then they paused to look at him. 'No, no,' he told them, 'I didn't come to trouble you. I came looking for someone . . . .'

He didn't see the cow anywhere in the forest. Didn't hear it cry either. But for the crickets and night birds all was silent. He grew anxious. 'The cry that I have been hearing all these nights seemed to come from this place. Even last night . . . .'

Suddenly he experienced an unknown fear. Had he imagined it all? His wife had always said, I don't hear any lowing. It's all your imagination. How could we ever hear a cry from that far? You imagine all sorts of things.

Can't be, he said to himself, I heard it quite distinctly. Heard the mother crying with fear and grief at being separated from her calf.

He turned and slowly walked back home. When Ram Singh asked, 'Saab, did you find the cow?' he stood there confused for a moment. When Ram Singh repeated the question, he started as if woken from sleep and said, 'No, no.'

'Saab, whose cow is it?'

'It's my cow. Mine.'

Ram Singh looked at him, surprised, 'Yours, saab?'

The company's rules did not permit anyone to have a cow inside the township. Ram Singh knew that. The watchman also knew that his saab didn't keep a cow, lawfully or otherwise. While Ram Singh stood there wondering, he walked on as if nothing had happened.

It was a busy day in the office. In addition to the routine jobs, he had to prepare answers for questions raised in Parliament and then have a sitting with the auditors. Later, he had to go to the port office twenty-five miles away, to get berths in the wharf for the company's ships waiting with cargo in the outer sea. None of this was difficult. He had a special knack for these jobs. But he knew that however hard he worked, he would never rise any further. He was aware of the reasons too. But there was nothing that he could do about it.

It was late morning before he telephoned his wife. 'Don't wait for me to have lunch. I have a meeting at the port. Can't say when

I'll be back.' His wife usually said 'OK' and put the receiver down. But he sensed that she had something to say that day.

'What is it?' he asked.

'She was here sometime ago.' Though his wife had only said *she*, he immediately understood whom she meant.

'Has she found the cow?' he asked eagerly.

'No. She wants us to make other . . . .'

'But didn't I tell you that in case she came I'd give her the money to buy another cow?'

'Yes, I told her that and she started crying. Said she would never buy another cow.'

He had expected this. But it disturbed him nevertheless.

'Can I ask you a question?' she asked. 'Suppose she comes to tell us that she has decided to buy a new cow after all and wants to borrow the money, will you give it to her? Of course, it's not *my* money. But you realise don't you, that its only a few months more to your retirement. Do you think she'll be able to return the money by then?'

He muttered something and put down the receiver. He saw his mother — shrunken, shrivelled, slightly stooped, a worn-out mundu over the shoulders a milk can in hand, walking along the footpath, not hurting even the grass on the road . . . .

Sometimes she came to the back of the house to say, 'Milk is in short supply today.' Or, 'No milk today. The calf . . .' and his wife would get angry. 'In that case, we shall make other arrangements.' And he would assure the woman, 'It doesn't matter! It's only for a day, isn't it?' Later, he would tell his wife, 'She could have added water and supplied us the milk. But she didn't. And anyway, if we don't get milk for a day, it's not the end of the world.' But his wife never seemed to understand him.

He always thought of his mother at such times. She had cared not only for her own children but for those of others too. She sold milk to make a living but she never traded her cows. She had made him understand the difference between the two at a very young age. Truth went before his mother like a burning wheel of fire, always, wherever she went.

It was quite late when he returned from the port office. He was alone with the driver in the car. He wished to say these things aloud to someone. On an impulse he addressed the driver. 'Raghavan Nair!'

This was a driver whom he had himself appointed many years ago.

The driver slowed down the car. 'Sir?'

'No, no, don't stop. I was just thinking.'

'Sir?'

'What does your mother do now, Raghavan Nair?'

'Sir, she's at home in our village.'

'How is her health?'

'Fine sir, just a little rheumatic trouble now and then. But not much to talk about.'

Then he asked, 'Do you have cows?'

'We only have five cents of land, sir. How can we keep cows there?'

He could not say anything more.

When he came home and his wife said, 'Shouldn't we make some other arrangement for milk?' he only said, 'Hmm.' He went out as if going for a walk. He walked fast up to the paan shop on the bank of the canal outside the township. But he stopped there confused. The road branched off in three directions. He was not sure which one he should take. On some mornings he had seen her coming that way. But he did not stop there for long.

The tired rays of the evening sun lay on the sluggish water. He walked eastward along the banks of the canal. Before him, showing him the way, was a wheel of fire moving very slowly.

NAGADDHUYYA

ARUN MHATRE

nominated by Vilas Sarang
translated by P.A. Kolharkar

I t has warmed up, he thought, as he came out of the newspaper office.

He looked at his watch. It was ten past eleven.

What! I was in there only for five minutes? He felt kind of insulted. Mr. Phadnis did not speak with me as he usually does, he thought. Mr. Bhagwat too had waved a distant acknowledgement. Was he really busy? Or was he just waving me off?

Things were getting unnecessarily tangled. He decided to stop thinking. He walked as if suspended in space, not a thought in his head.

The station was left far behind. Now it was shops and showcases

Nagaddhuyya (title of the original story) was first published in Marathi in *Anushthub* Diwali Issue, 1989.

stocked with the latest toys. A busy congested locality.

He felt a little better, even in his present mood. Good! Even if nothing else can be managed, I can at least spend some time on my way back looking at these shops with their strange assortment of toys.

He did not know when he reached the beach. For no apparent reason he found himself walking faster. He walked, as if seeking refuge, till he was quite close to the sea.

There were about a dozen people sleeping there, scattered all over the shade of the seaside arch. There was a time when he had felt pity for such people. He had wanted to print their photographs in newspapers captioned with lines from his own poetry — to show the world how mercurially alive was his own socio-economic awareness.

But it was different today. 'They have ruined the city!' he muttered to himself as he looked around for a patch of shade on the parapet.

About a dozen launches stood yawning close by the beach. Their bright-coloured flags shimmered in the sun. The water around them was stained blue-black with diesel.

The scorched, stagnant stench of the sea irritated his nostrils. He placed his bag on a stone chair that was nearby, and rested his bottom on the parapet, watching the frightened doves as they shuffled away. The parapet was now in the shade but the sun had baked it red hot. It hurt. Yet he sat there, suffering as though he were a fit candidate for branding. He knew he was angry. But he didn't know with whom or why and this only made him feel more angry.

The arch on the beach was the city's pride and once upon a time, he had devoted many hours appreciating the artistic pillars with their beautiful carving. Today he found himself spending more time looking at the men who lay sprawled all around him.

The day wore on and as the shadow of the arch crept away and the sun fell directly on him, he felt more and more annoyed.

'Lazy bums! Wherever you look, you find them sprawling. Loafers! Go, get back to your villages!' he muttered as if reading out from an editorial.

As he looked, the whole city seemed to become smaller and smaller till it was no bigger than a little island drawn on the pages of a geography text book. He could clearly see men wriggling like worms on the edge of its shore.

He wrinkled his nose in disgust. He could not move away from the beach. He continued to sit there by the sea, vehemently protesting against all that he saw.

Am I hungry?

May be ... may be not ... probably not .... Good! that cuts down on expenses.

Thirsty?

A bit ... just a l-i-t-t-l-e ... but can manage.

Do I want a cigarette?

Not now. After a while. Maybe.

Are my eyes turning more frequently to the passing women than to the men?

Yes, perhaps yes .... Oh my God!

He was puzzled. What is it exactly that I want at this moment?

He unrolled a list of his wants before his eyes, in order of priority. He caressed each one tenderly. As if touching a little child's silken head ... But there were no answers there. Things he desired appeared alongside other things that he didn't really want at this moment. He was confused.

Suddenly, intensely, he could think of only one thing .... I am unemployed.

He felt insecure — like a commuter entering a station without a ticket.

Job? What the hell is a job? What is that thing called a job?

A big fat cross on the attendance sheet, cutting through columns and columns of days?

One HUGE cross on every page! A grey cross! All over the page.

A cross racing over the pages . . . page after page after . . . page . . . till no pages are left!

Cross after cross . . . lines of crosses . . . closely-linked crosses . . . crisp crackling crosses!

And what's that sound coming from within them? Papers? Files? Fingers? Currency notes?

A trickle of sweat makes its indifferent journey from hair to forehead.

Is that the sound I hear?

What is that sound coming from inside me?

He brought out a diary from his shirt pocket. It was full of jottings, altogether of a different sort.

No. A job is not a cross blocking the lines in a diary. A job only beheads days. Snaps them off. A signature a day, in the morning on the muster, and one head severed. One happy, happy head severed and we are ready to spread ourselves thin through the length of the day.

Yes, a job is a sword . . . a sword that mercilessly slashes the days.

He paused. He was aware that his thoughts kept returning to this lost sword.

How did I come to lose it? No, it's not lost. Somebody snatched it away. Who?

Again and again, without any rhyme or reason, his mind returned to the violence between the two factions of the factory union. The heap of soda bottles, the arrests, the fights, the pullings and tuggings, the police sirens performing a post-mortem on the atmosphere, a strained timid phone call to a neighbour, the surreptitious trip in a group to the factory the next day, the shock valiantly swallowed on seeing the locked gate and the notice (signed by the owner), the retreat from the gate, from the eyes of the police, the rank abuses mushrooming in the mind, the frightened body, the shattered relationship between the employer and the employed. All this he remembered. As if it had just happened.

Well, the doors of the fort are shut and the rope has been drawn in.

Let us bring a new rope. Tie it stealthily! Scale the fort!

Who will bring the rope? Me? No! No!

The owner? No, no! Certainly not. The leader? NO! No one at all . . . ? How is it possible? Surely somebody will bring the rope! After all this is a Democracy, brother! Not a joke! Everything runs according to the Rule of Law. Do you understand that? The rule of law, not the law of the jungle. Yes. But when? When? When?

He was tired.

Remembering Phadnis and Bhagwat made him angry with himself.

Damn it, he told himself. A lock-out does not mean I have lost a leg under a local train. Why do I have to talk to all and sundry? I'm ready to spill my guts just for a song. Why did I talk to Mr. Phadnis — every detail spiced and seasoned? To impress him? To steal sympathy from him? It's a drink really! A cupful of sympathy! First a cutting — a half-cup — of tea and then, to top it, a cupful of sympathy! Drink it up man and then kick yourself in your pants — for being summarily thrown out.

He remembered Mr. Phadnis once again.

Did he really throw me out? Yes, that's what he did. That's right . . . Of course, he did!

Where is my sword . . . ? Where is it?

Suddenly he thought he was being stripped naked. Stark naked. He looked all around him. Nobody was looking in his direction. Absolutely nobody. He felt relieved. Somehow sad.

Hell! Am I related to these sleeping earthworms? A relative of these forehead-scratching refugees? Ha!

Shorn of a job, I am naked. *A complete nagaddhuyya . . . nagaddhuyya . . . nagaddhuyya . . . Tak dina dhin!*

He got up briskly and started walking.

Now he realised that he had been sitting in the sun. Directly under the sun. Walking, he felt himself immediately become part of the road. He felt relieved. 'They have ruined the city!' he hissed, looking at the sprawling men. They made him feel that he was quite different from them.

As he turned towards the teastall, he reminded himself that he was merely enjoying compulsory leave.

'One cutting of tea!' (and no sympathy please!) 'Make it quick and hot!'

'Sixty paise, Saab. In coins!'

'Its gone up to sixty, has it?'

'All right! Give fifty.'

'Here, take the sixty.' No sympathy . . . no more bowlfuls of sympathy!

He gulped down all his anger with the tea.

'Bhai, one Four Square.'

'How many?'

'I said one, only one. Can I smoke four at a time?' he asked in irritation. He lighted the cigarette, inhaling in that one puff, everything around him and then, his neck bent low, he quickly marched away.

By the time he realized that he was walking too fast and had also finished his cigarette, he was at the traffic crossing in the centre of the city and far away from the sea. He was rather embarrassed to see the signals, vehicles rushing fender-to-fender, the traffic, the police. This was a very different scene from the thoughts coursing through his mind. He stopped as if gasping for breath. Where was he to go now?

Only an hour gone. Only an hour? Yes. Only one hour. The afternoon is barking. Sweat, cutting through the eyebrows, creeps like an insect through the hair. His face has become oily. And through it all, what gleams sharp and metal-like is the fact that he is Unemployed. It frightened him.

Now the bank staff will come out for lunch. They will see me. Will enquire solicitously. I will have to tell them everything. They will fill the bowls of sympathy, pour over me a trickle of consolation. Ask questions. Drench me copiously. Immerse and pull me out of a half-cup of tea. Fill their mouths with paan talking all the time about me and spray their spittle all over me.

Where is my sword? Where is it?

His heart began to beat faster. Somehow he must slip out of that place. As soon as the traffic light changed, he crossed the road rapidly and began to run across the maidan. As if somebody was chasing him, stalking him from behind . . . from the flanks . . . up front . . . . Ducking his head, he ran madly. Where was he to go? To the sea again? The railway station? The theatre? Towards that road? Or the road beyond? Or even beyond that? Where?

It was four months since the factory had closed. But in that one moment he experienced the misery of all those four months. All those months of wandering—on the roads, in buses, out of his home. For four months I have laid myself out flat like a road . . . a road to nowhere . . . . A skybound road.

For some time he stood before a poster. He read all the names on it. Saw all the pictures.

And suddenly thought of Tomorrow. God! To be confronted by yet another naked day? A naked tomorrow. The seminal representative of all the naked days gone by. Without eyes. With elongated arms . . . naked . . . . What can I offer it? That is the only difference between me and all these scurrying people around me. They don't have a tomorrow waiting to swallow them up. They don't have a tomorrow demanding a sacrifice (and some money, if I can spare it).

Yes. That is the only difference. Time crawls behind them. And they're fleeing. While I'm bent under the burden of Today. The thought of Tomorrow upsets me. The Day after tomorrow frightens me.

He wanted to go home at once, though it would be a shame to return so early. He was quite fed up of rolling like a football through the lanes and the alleys of the city till His Highness, the Sun completed his rounds.

'Move, Sun, move . . . move on fast,' he muttered looking at the poster. He saw a procession coming from the opposite direction. Slogan-shouting strangers.

It was a rally made of innumerable strangers. Should I join it? But he felt cheated when the rally came close to him. He thought he could spot some familiar faces. Damn it! Do the same people rally around each day but under a different banner? Perhaps the jobless chaps from his union took part in the rally as leaders . . . . Get away from here, come on! Quick, he warned himself.

He saw a small garden behind a government building. He quickly walked up to it. There were a few people in the garden. A couple of men were lying on the lawn in the shade. A man was munching chana as he read a newspaper. No one else.

He plonked himself down, sat crosslegged. He heard his knee-bones crack. He stretched his legs and deliberately cracked his ankle bone.

He could not see the road because of the hedge in front of him. He could hear slogans but couldn't see the rallyists either. A good place to hide, he thought as he put his hands behind him and reclined on them. The ground was rather uneven but it didn't matter. The clickety-clack of trains and scattered bits of rhythmic slogans filtered through the hedge.

His eyes went skimming over the hedge. He could see only the taller buildings. There was peace there, floating at some higher, unreachable level. He flew out of his body and began to think of the city that rises to seventeen floors.

What is the chemistry of a city that speaks garrulously through the clatter of traffic?

He saw the harsh net that connected all the clock-towers. It was hanging right over his heart. He saw himself offering puja to the net with all the fervour he could muster. He had surrendered himself completely to the call of the end-of-shift siren. And he was still naked. A nagaddhuyya. But he imagined that he saw the city spread a striped mesh over his body, to cover him. The city teeming with the jobless. The city that could weave together the unemployed and the employed. The city that covers itself with a crowd. The city seated in a deep trance, wrapped in its shawl of shrill sounds.

A flock of white birds suddenly came into view. They flew across the sky towards the sea. The air in the seventeenth floor must now be warm. The chemical concoction of the city came to life and moved upward like a bubble and filled the seventeen floors. Up to the brim.

The city happened to notice him. The city noted that he was watching it. It felt that it should hold his hand and help him rise, make him wipe his eyes, tell him to brush off the grass stuck to his bottom, take him into the nearby station and push him into the colourless crowd of commuters.

Then at least he would forget that he was naked. Become part of the crowd.

But the city too was indolent. Besides, it had taught itself not to pamper anybody. It stayed hung on the washing line, beside the underwear drying on the seventeenth floor.

The inaudible tick-tock of the tower clock spread over his forehead like a balm.

The city let him snore peacefully on its beating heart. In his childlike nakedness.

REFLOWERING

SUNDARA RAMASWAMY

nominated and translated by
S. Krishnan

Amma was lying on the cot and I was curled up on the floor right next to it. Amma and I were free to get up as late as we pleased. We had made it our habit over the years. We had to put up a battle of sorts to win it. Ours is a family that takes pride in the fact that we safeguard the dharma of the early riser: for generations now, we've all bathed before sunrise. But then, Amma and I were invalids. Amma had asthma and I suffered from joint pains. Both could create problems early in the morning.

Outside, there were sounds of the horse shaking its mane, of its bells jangling. The horse buggy was ready. This meant that Appa had picked up the bunch of keys for his shop. It also meant that the

'Vikasham' ('Reflowering') was first published in the Tamil edition of *India Today*, Jan 31 - Feb 5, 1990.

clock was inching towards eight-thirty. He would now put on his slippers. *Kweech. Kweech.* Then, once downstairs, the abrupt impatient sound of the umbrella opening, closing. The daily umbrella-health-test, that.

The door opened slightly. A thin streak of sunlight pranced into the room, a shifting glass-pipe of light, dust swirling inside it. Appa! I see him in profile — one eye, spectacles, half a forehead streaked with vibhuti and a dot of chandanam paste, golden-yellow, topped by a vivid spot of red kumkumam.

'Boy! Ambi! Get up!' Appa said.

I closed my eyes. I did not move a limb. As if I were held captive by deep sleep.

'Ai! Get up. You good-for-nothing,' Amma said. 'Appa's calling.'

On the sly I looked at Appa. He looked affectionate, even gentle. As if I were being roused from heavy slumber, I opened my eyes with pretended difficulty.

'Get ready, Ambi. Eat and then go to Aanaipaalam,' said Appa. 'Go and bring Rowther to the shop straightaway. I'll send the buggy back for you.'

I looked at Appa, then at Amma. I had told her about the squabble between Appa and Rowther in the shop the previous day.

'Can you or can you not manage without him?' asked Amma. 'This farce has gone on far too long,' she said. 'Making up one day and parting the next!'

Appa's face reddened. It seemed as if, if it grew any redder, blood might start dribbling from the tip of his nose.

'Onam is round the corner. *You* can come to the shop and make the bills,' he screamed. Anger twisted his lips, slurred and flattened out the words.

'Is Rowther the only person in this whole world who knows how to make bills?' asked Amma.

'Shut your mouth!' yelled Appa. Abruptly he turned to me. 'Get up, you!' he ordered.

I sprang up from my bed and stood taut as a strung bow.

'Go. Do what I told you to,' he growled.

As if someone unseen had tugged at the wheels attached to my feet, I moved swiftly out of the room.

I heard the horse buggy leave the house.

I got ready in double quick time. What briskness! I wore — as I usually didn't — a dhoti over my halfpants, and a full-sleeved shirt, all in the hope that it would make me speak up with some confidence. I didn't feel my usual anger with Appa. I didn't feel sad either. It seemed as if even some little fondness seeped through. Poor thing! He had got himself into a fix. On an impulse, he'd spoken harshly to Rowther. He could have been more calm. Now, if a person is merely short-tempered, one can talk of calmness. But if he is *anger personified*?

Excited by this paradox, I went and stood before Amma. I looked her straight in the face and I said, 'If he is anger personified where is the question of calmness?' Amma laughed; almost at once, she made her face stern and, 'Smart, aren't you?' she asked. 'Now, if you are a clever boy, you'll go take Rowther to the shop.' Placing her right hand over her heart she said, 'Tell him whatever *he* may have said, I apologise for it.'

I went and climbed into the buggy.

I too thought that we could not manage the Onam festival sales without Rowther. Who could do sums like him? He was lightning quick in mental arithmetic. Five people sitting in a row, with paper and pencils, would not be equal to one Rowther and his brain. Remarkable. Even regular buyers who flocked round him to have their bills tallied were amazed. 'Is this a mere human brain?' many wondered aloud. 'If the man can be this fast just by listening to the figures, what would he not do if he'd been granted sight?' And to think that Rowther has only studied up to the third class. That's two grades less than Gomathi who works in the shop, fetching and cleaning.

The dispute between Appa and Rowther had started mildly enough the previous evening. 'Look here, Rowther, what are you going to do if you let your debts keep mounting like this?' Appa asked. Rowther had chosen all the clothes he wanted, piled them up by his side, before thinking of asking Appa for credit. It was quite clear that Appa did not like this.

'What can I do, Ayyah? My house is full of women. My sons are useless. My sons-in-law are useless. Four sons, four daughters-in-law, eight granddaughters, eight grandsons. How many is that? Just one piece of cloth each, and the cost goes up.'

Appa was staring at Rowther, as if thinking, The man is getting out of hand. I must cut him to size. Right away.

'Kolappa, wrap up the clothes and give me the bill,' said Rowther.

How dare he take the things before permission had been granted? Appa's face reddened. 'It is not possible for me to give you credit this time,' he said.

'So, you're saying you don't want our relationship to continue, no, Ayyah? All right. Girl, take me home.'

Rowther stood up. Gomathi took his right arm and placed it on her left shoulder. They went down the steps. When the shop closed in the evening, he would usually look in the direction of my father and take permission to leave. That particular evening he did not take permission. That is, he had taken leave.

I thought I would first pick up Gomathi and take her with me to Rowther's house. That would perhaps lessen his hurt. But Gomathi was not at home. 'Rowther had sent word that he was not coming. She's just left for the shop,' her mother said.

I took a shortcut through the grove, and reached Rowther's house through a narrow lane. A tiled house, the roof low. In the front yard there was a well on the right hand side, its parapet wall, stark, unpainted, broken. Velvet moss sprang around it in bright patches. Stone steps led to the house. A strip of gunny bag hung from the main door.

'It's me, Ambi!' I announced my arrival loudly.

A little girl came out followed by another who was obviously her twin.

'Who is it, child?' came Rowther's voice from inside the house.

'It's me. Ambi,' I said.

'Come! Come,' said Rowther. His voice bubbled with happiness.

I pushed aside the sack curtain and went inside. The floor had been swabbed smooth with cowdung. Rowther was sitting cross-legged, like a lord. His arms reached out for me. 'Come, come,' his mouth kept saying.

I went and knelt in front of him. He put his arms around me. His eyes stared and stared, as if trying to recapture the vision they had lost long ago. He pressed me down by my shoulders, dragged me towards him and sat me down beside him. His emotions seemed to overwhelm him.

'Ah! You seem to be wearing a dhoti today!' he said.

'Just felt like it.'

'What's the border like?'

'Five-striped.'

'Just like Ayyah, uhn? The boys in the shop tell me that you look just like your father, too. It is my misfortune that I can't see you.'

He ran his fingers over my face, my nose, my mouth, my neck, my eyes, my ears, my forehead. 'Everything in place, thank the Lord.' He laughed.

I thought that this was the right moment to tell him why I had come. But words stuck in my throat, as if held there by an unseen hand.

'Amma . . .' I started to say, making a tentative start.

Rowther interrupted me. 'How is madam's health now?'

'As usual.'

'I have *Thuthuvalai, Khandankattri leghiyam*. No better medicine for asthma. Only, Ayyah likes to see English labels on his medicine bottles. I don't have English here. Only medicines,' he said, enjoying his own joke hugely.

This was the right moment to tackle him.

'Amma wants me to take you to the shop. She wants me to tell you that *she* is very sorry if Appa has said anything to hurt you. You are not to misunderstand him. She says please don't turn down her request.'

Rowther's face visibly brightened. He raised his hands in salute. 'Mother, you are a great woman,' he called out. 'Get up, let's go to the shop at once,' he said.

That year the sales during Onam were very good. Rowther was in his element. With great elan he supervised the shopboys who constantly jostled around him. He looked like Abhimanyu in the Mahabharata fighting a whole battalion, single-handedly. He would state the price as soon as the cost and quantity of the material were mentioned to him. Only the good Lord knew what spark it was in his brain, what genius that did not need even a minute to calculate? A brain that could multiply and total up the cost of sixteen different items in a trice to announce, 'Item sixteen. Grand total — 1414 rupees 25 paise,' how could that be called an average brain? Even if the whole thing were written down on the blackboard, I would have easily taken half an hour to work it out. But for him, answers slipped forth like lightning. He had never till now made a single mistake. Amma has told me that in the early years of their association, Appa used to sit up half the night, checking Rowther's calculations. It seems he'd say, 'That man is getting beside himself. I must find at least an error or two.' But he never could. He just lost a good night's sleep.

One day, a cart drawn by a single bullock, heavily curtained on both sides, stopped in front of the shop. From inside came the wailing of women and children.

'Sounds like the females from my household,' Rowther said.

Rowther's house had come up for public auction! Apparently the amina was taking all the household things and flinging them on to the street.

Rowther started crying like a child and called on God to help him out. Even as he was emoting, Kolappan came with a bill saying, '45 metres and 70 centimetres at 13 rupees and 45 paise.' Rowther stopped his keening for a moment and said to him, 'Write this down, 614 rupees and 66 paise.' He turned to my father who was at the cash-counter and sobbed. 'Ayyah. I have to pay the court the loan and the interest on it, more than five thousand rupees. Where will I go for the money?'

Appa took Rowther in the horse buggy to seé a lawyer.

Rowther did not show up for work the next day. Kolappan said he had with his own eyes seen Rowther, reciting the bills in Chettiar's cloth shop.

'What injustice! I have just come back after paying the court the entire amount for his debts. He's let me down, the ungrateful wretch!' Appa shouted.

The shop assistant Kolappan also whipped himself into a fury. 'He knows how to calculate, but he's a senseless idiot. Wait, I'll go this minute and drag him here by his hair,' he said as he jumped onto his bicycle.

Appa sat down on the floor, devastated. He started to mumble. 'This is a wicked world,' he said. 'These days you can't even trust your own mother.'

In a little while, Kolappan returned. Rowther was sitting behind him, on the carrier. He marched a stonelike Rowther to the cash-counter.

'I lost my head, Ayyah,' said Rowther as he stood before Appa, his hands folded in supplication.

'A time will come when you will be cut down to size,' said Appa.

'Please don't say such things, Ayyah,' pleaded Rowther. 'Come work for me and I'll pay your debts, the Chettiar said. And I lost my head.'

Appa only repeated, 'The time will come when you will be cut down to size.'

And, surprise of surprises, things soon happened that made it look as if Appa was going to be right after all. When Appa returned from Bombay that year after seeing his wholesalers, he brought back a small machine and showed it to Amma. 'This can do calculations,' he said.

'A machine?'

'It can.'

Amma made up a sum. Appa pressed a few keys. The machine gave the answer.

I quickly worked it out on a piece of paper. 'The answer is correct, Amma!' I shouted.

'Have they transformed Rowther's brain into a machine?' asked my mother.

That whole day I kept trying out the calculator. That night, I kept it by my side when I slept. I gave it the most difficult sums I could think of. Its every answer was right. I remembered something Gomathi had once told me. 'Thatha! How can you do sums in a *nimit?*' she had asked Rowther, mixing up as she always did, the Tamil and the common English word. It seems Rowther had said, 'Child, I have three extra nerves in my brain.' Now, how did those extra nerves get inside this machine? I couldn't control my excitement.

I showed the calculator to Gomathi. She also worked out many many sums.

'Even I am getting it all right,' she said, 'this machine is more cunning than Thatha!'

One evening Rowther was totalling up for the day. Gomathi was sitting there, the calculator balanced on her lap, checking out his calculations. At one point, very impulsively she said, 'You are correct, Thatha.'

'Are you telling me I am right?' asked Rowther.

'I have worked it out,' said Gomathi.

'Hmm,' said Rowther. 'I'll give you a sum. Answer.'

Rowther gave her a sum. Gomathi gave the right answer. He tried sum after sum on her. She had the correct answer each time.

Rowther turned pale. 'Dear God. I am so dumb I cannot understand anything,' he muttered.

'I'm not doing the sums, Thatha,' said Gomathi. 'It's the machine.'

She stuffed the calculator into his hands.

Rowther's hands shook as he took the calculator. His fingers trembled. He touched the whole front portion of the calculator, the whole back.

'Is *this* doing the sums?' he asked again.

'Yes,' said Gomathi.

'You keep it yourself,' he said as he thrust it back at her.

After this, Rowther was a very quiet man indeed. Words failed him. He remained in a state of stupor, leaning against the wall. That day, Gomathi and I took care of all the billing. After a long time, Gomathi dug her finger into his thigh and asked, 'Thatha, why don't you say something, Thatha?' But he said nothing even to that.

He kept coming to the shop regularly but he looked and acted like a walking corpse. It seemed as if all the laughter, happiness, backchat, teasing, sarcasm, had dropped off him. His voice was slow, hesitant. Even his body looked thinner.

Appa had stopped asking him to do the bills.

One afternoon, it was a busy time in the shop. Murugan had a pile of cut pieces with him. I was working out the cost. Suddenly, Rowther interrupted him, 'What did you say was the price of poplin?'

Murugan stopped calling out and looked at Rowther's face, '15 rupees and 10 paise per metre.'

'Wrong. Get the material out and look — it is 16 rupees and 10 paise per metre.'

Appa got up. He came and stood next to Rowther.

Murugan's face fell as he checked the price. 'You are right,' he mumbled.

'You have sold ten metres. You could have lost ten rupees. Are you here to give away Ayyah's money to everyone who comes in from the street?'

'So, you know the price?' Appa asked Rowther.

'Only a memory, Ayyah.'

'Do you remember all the prices?'

'It is God's will,' said Rowther.

'What is the price of the smallest towel then?' asked Appa.

'Four rupees and 10 paise.'

'And the biggest one?'

'Thirty-six rupees and 40 paise.'

Appa kept on asking. The answers kept coming.

Appa looked amazed. He could not believe his ears. He took a deep breath. He could not help doing so.

'If that's so, you do one thing. When bills are being made, please check the prices.'

'I will do my best, Ayyah,' said Rowther. Then he looked up and said, 'Oh, by the way, have you paid your electricity bill, Ayyah? Today is the last date for payment.'

'Oh, no!' said Appa, calling out to Kollappan.

Rowther said, 'He hasn't come today, Ayyah.'

'How do you know?' asked Appa.

'Everybody has a voice, a smell. Today I missed Kolappan's voice, his smell,' said Rowther, and then he called out to Murugan.

'Yesterday he told a customer that we had no double dhotis. Please reprimand him,' Rowther said.

'I don't understand,' said Appa.

'Ayyah. You put out ten double dhotis for sale. Weren't only seven sold? There should be three remaining, shouldn't there?'

Appa asked for the dhotis to be brought.

Sure enough there were three unsold.

Rowther let a sardonic smile play on his face. He said to Murugan, 'Oh Lord Muruga, you merrily send customers away by telling them we don't have what we do actually have. Are we here for business or for charity?'

That evening Rowther moved away from the bill-making section and went and sat closer to Appa.

'If I am by your side I will be more helpful, Ayyah,' he said and without missing a beat, 'and if you increase the speed of the fan a little, yours truly will also get some breeze.'

Appa gave the appropriate order.

'It is time to pay your advance income tax, sir. Shouldn't you see your auditor?' asked Rowther.

'Yes, I must go see him,' said Appa.

It was time to close the shop.

'Ayyah, you had wanted to get some medicine for madam. Have you bought it, yet?'

'I'll buy it.'

Appa was tugging at the locks to check if they had been locked properly.

'Ayyah, you were saying that your mother's tithi was due soon. Why not ask Murugan to notify the priest on his way home?'

'Good idea,' said Appa.

The employees left one by one.

Gomathi took Rowther's hand, placed it on her shoulder and started moving.

'Won't you be doing the bills any more, Thatha?'

'Ibrahim Hassan Rowther is no longer a mere adding machine. He is now the manager. It is God's will,' Rowther replied.

THE CONTRIBUTORS

M. ASADUDDIN is a Reader in the Department of English at the Jamia Millia Islamia University, New Delhi. He translates frequently from and to Bangla, Urdu, Hindi and English.

CHANDRIKA BALAN is the author of several short stories and one novelette in Malayalam and has translated Thakazhi and Lalithambika Antarjanam into English. She is a Professor of English at All Saints College, Trivandrum, and is currently engaged in an UGC research project on 'The Woman and the Family in Indian English Drama.'

RIMLI BHATTACHARYA is a comparatist by training. She taught English at the Centre for Linguistics and English at Jawaharlal Nehru University for some years. She is currently engaged in a research project on 19th century stage actresses of Bengal.

BHUPENDRANARAYAN BHATTACHARYYA is a painter and short story writer based in Guwahati. He has received several awards for his short stories which have been translated from Assamese into Hindi. Five of his stories have also been selected for the first Assamese television serial.

RANJITA BISWAS is a freelance journalist and creative writer. She has translated extensively from Assamese and Bangla into English and vice versa. Her translation of Bhabendranath Saikia's novel, *Antareep*, has appeared in *Prachi*, a Sahitya Akademi compilation.

ENAKSHI CHATTERJEE is a writer, translator and media critic. She translates from Bangla to English and vice versa. She has translated a wide range of Bangla novels and has published over 30 books on science and science fiction; *Paramanu Jijnasa* written jointly with her husband, Santimoy Chatterjee won her the Rabindra Puroshkar.

DILIP PURUSHOTTAM CHITRE is known primarily as a poet in Marathi and English. Among his many publications is an award-winning collection of short stories. Chitre also writes plays and screenplays. His Hindi feature film, *Godam* was awarded the Jury's Special Prize at the Nantes Film Festival in 1983.

GEETA DHARMARAJAN is a writer for children and adults. Her books have been published by Rupa & Co, National Book Trust and Affiliated East-West Press, Ltd; five have been translated into Bangla. A Children's Book Trust (CBT) prize-winning book and a collection of stories by Indian women, edited by her, are slated for publication. She edits a health and activity magazine for children called *Tamasha!* and is the executive director of Katha.

INDIRA GOSWAMI is the author of many novels and short stories, some of which have been translated from Assamese into English, Hindi, and Malayalam. She received the Sahitya Akademi Award in 1983 for her novel, *Mamare Dhara Tamoval*. Her *Adha Lekha Dastavi* (1988) was translated recently into English. She is also a translator and literary critic. At present she teaches in the Department of Modern Indian Languages at Delhi University.

SARAH JOSEPH is the author of several collections of stories including *Papathara* and *Kadinte Sangeetham* and the novel *Nanmathinmakalude Vriksham*. An activist, she formed the first feminist theatre group in Kerala and has directed Stree, an anti-dowry play. She is currently Professor of Malayalam in the Government Victoria College, Palghat.

FAKIR MUHAMMED KATPADI is actively associated with Samudaya, a radical-progressive cultural movement in Karnataka. His publications include *Ghori Katti* a collection of short stories, the novel *Sarakugalu* (1989) and the travelogue, *Keraladalli Handinaidu Dinagalu* (1989). His latest work *Kayyoorina Raita Veeraru*, a work of historical research, is to be published this year.

SUHAS GOLE has taught English at Patkar College, Bombay for over 25 years. His translations of the poems of Dalit poet Namdeo Dhasal have appeared in *The Bombay Literary Review*.

S. KRISHNAN, translator and journalist, has served as Cultural Adviser to the United States Information Service for several years. He is a regular contributor to a number of Indian and foreign journals. A book-reviewer and occasional poet, Krishnan is a senior editor of *Sruti*, a Madras-based magazine of music and dance.

P.A. KOLHARKAR retired as Head of the Department of English,

B.N.N. College, Bhiwandi, Maharastra. He is now engaged in translating fiction from Marathi to English.

SARAT KUMAR MUKHOPADHYAY is a major Bangla poet, critic and fiction writer who at one time also wrote under the pseudonym of Trishanku. Presently he is a counseller in the Creative Writing Programme of the Indira Gandhi National Open University in Calcutta. His latest collection of poetry, *Shrestha Kavita* was published in 1985 and a collection of his short stories entitled *Shreshtha Galpa* was published in 1991.

K. AYYAPPA PANIKER is a major poet and critic in Malayalam. Among other awards, he has won the Kerala Sahitya Akademi Awards for poetry (1975) and criticism (1983) and the Sahitya Akademi Award for poetry (1984). He was Professor of English at the University of Kerala and is currently the Chief Editor of Medieval Indian Literature, Sahitya Akademi.

T. PADMANABHAN was a pioneer of the new short story in Malayalam in the 1950s. He is one of the senior writers in Malayalam who has stayed with the short story. He is the author of several anthologies from which many stories have been translated into other Indian languages including English.

SURENDRA PRAKASH is the pen-name of Surendra Kumar Oberoi, Sahitya Akademi Award Winner for Urdu in 1989. Following the Partition he migrated to Delhi from Lahore and made his living as hawker, rickshaw-puller, flower-seller, and travelling salesman. His works include *Doosre Aadmi Ka Drawing Room* (1968), *Barf Par Makalma* (1980) and the award-winning anthology, *Baz Goyi* (1988). He now lives in Bombay and writes scripts for films and television plays.

VIJAYALAKSHMI QUERESHI is currently the Librarian at the Sahitya Akademi Library in New Delhi.

ANISUR RAHMAN is Reader in the Department of English, Jamia Millia Islamia, New Delhi. He has worked and published in the areas of Indo-English Literature, Comparative Studies and Literary Translation. He has widely translated from and to English and Urdu.

MADHURANTAKAM RAJARAM is a teacher by profession. He has won the Sahitya Akademi Best Story Award. Among his publications are the novels *Trisankudi Svargam* (1970), *Chinna Prapandcham - Sirivada* (1972) and four anthologies of short stories, *Tonu Veligenidmina Dipalu* (1966) *Vakragatulu Itara Kathalu* (1968), *Kamma Temmera* (1970) and *Punarnavam* (1970).

SUNDARA RAMASWAMY, a doyen among Tamil writers, is best known for his novel, *Oru Puliamaratthin Kathai*. He lives in the border area between Tamil Nadu and Kerala, which is reflected in his writings. He is also a poet and has received many literary awards, including that of the Sahitya Akademi.

VAKATI PANDURANGA RAO is an information professional with multimedia experience. He is the author of about 25 books, four of which are collections of short stories. His stories have been translated into many languages, including Russian. At home in Tamil, Telugu, Hindi and English, he has translated widely from and into these languages and has edited books for National Book Trust and the Sahitya Akademi. He is presently Deputy Editor of *Andhra Prabha Illustrated Weekly*.

K. RAGHAVENDRA RAO has taught Political Science at various Indian universities and is currently UGC Emeritus Fellow at the University of Mangalore. He has translated extensively both poetry and fiction from Kannada to English, including *Parva*, a novel by Bhyarappa.

REKHA has specialised in English Literature and is currently a professor in the English Department, University of Shimla. Her publications include *Apne Hissay Ki Dhoop*, and *Chindi-Chindi Sukh*, a short story collection.

VILAS SARANG is a short story writer and poet. His stories have been widely published. A collection in French translation appeared before Penguin India brought out his *Fair Tree of the Void* (1990). He has also published collections of poems in English and Marathi and a book on translation theory in English. He has taught in Iraq for several years, and is now Professor and Head of the English Department at Bombay University.

ASHOK SRINIVASAN is Editor of *Indian Horizons*, a publication of the Indian Council for Cultural Relations (ICCR). He is a writer of short fiction in English.

R.S. SUDARSHANAM taught English until his retirement. He is a novelist, short story writer and literary critic in Telugu. His novel *Samsara Vriksham*, has been translated into Hindi and Gujarati. He has translated extensively from English to Telugu and vice versa

SWAMI is the pen-name of Bandi Narayana Swami. He teaches in a single-teacher school in a small village near Kamalapuram in Cuddapah District of Andhra Pradesh. He is not a prolific writer — publishing hardly one or two stories in a year — but his stories have carved a niche for themselves in Telugu literature. His story, 'The Rains did not Come,' won the first prize in the Ugadi Competition of *Andhra Prabha Illustrated Weekly* in 1991. He is closely associated with the Anantapur Writers' Club which is infusing freshness and excitement into the Telugu short story.

PURNA CHANDRA TEJASVI lives in his coffee estate in Karnataka. One of the major writers of the Navya School, he has since moved away from it. He is amongst the foremost litterateurs of Karnataka and is known as a poet, playwright and fiction writer. *Huliyurina Sarahaddu* and *Abachoorina Post-offisu* are two of his important short story collections. His works have been made into films and have been extensively translated into other Indian languages.

RUTH VANITA teaches English literature at Miranda House, Delhi University. She has published poetry in English and has translated fiction and verse from Hindi to English for *Manushi: a Journal about Women and Society*. She is co-editor of *In Search of Answers: Voices from the first five years of Manushi*, published by Zed Books (1984).

RAJENDRA YADAV, an eminent writer of the *Nai Kahani* movement in post-Independence Hindi fiction, is also a critic and translator. His stories and novels have been translated into Indian and non-Indian languages and have been made into films, tele-films and plays. He is currently the editor of *Hans*, a Hindi literary journal.

SELECT BIBLIOGRAPHY

Assamese

Ajir Ahom Prantik, Silpukhuri, Guwahati 780003.
Sutradhar, Manjeera House, Motilal Nehru Road, Guwahati 780001.
Asam Bani (Special Issue), Tribune Building, Guwahati.
Dainik Asam (Puja Special), Gopinath Nagar, Guwahati 780016.
Prakash, (Special Issue) Publication Board of Assam, Guwahati.

Bangla

Aaj Kaal, 96, Raja Rammohan Sarani, Calcutta 700009.
Ananda Bazar Patrika, 6 Prafulla Sarkar Street, Calcutta 700001.
Desh, Prafulla Sarkar Street, Calcutta 700001.
Jugantar, 41A, Acharya J.C.Bose Rd., Calcutta 700017.
Khela (Puja Supplement), 96, Raja Rammohan Sarani, Calcutta 700009.
Pratikshana, 7, Jawahar Lal Nehru Rd., Calcutta 700013.

English

The Deccan Herald, 66, M.G. Road, Bangalore 560001.
The Hindustan Times, Kasturba Gandhi Marg, New Delhi 110001.
The Illustrated Weekly of India, Bennet Coleman & Co., Bombay 400001.
Indian Literature, Sahitya Akademi, Rabindra Bhavan, New Delhi 110001.
Indian Express, Express Building, Bahadur Shah Zafar Marg, New Delhi 110002.
New Quest, Indian Association for Cultural Freedom, 850/8A Shivaji Nagar, Pune 411004.
The Times of India, Bahadurshah Zafar Marg, New Delhi 110002.

Hindi

Dastavej, Visvanath Tiwari, Bethia Hatha, Gorakhpur, U.P.
Hans, 2/36, Ansari Road, Daryaganj, New Delhi 110002.
Indraprastha Bharati, Hindi Akademi, A-26/23, Sunlight Insurance Bldg.,

Asaf Ali Road, New Delhi 110002.
Kathya Roop, 224, Tularam Bagh, Allahabad 211006.
Madhumati, Rajasthan Sahitya Akademi, Udaipur.
Pahal 763 Agarwal Colony, Jabalpur, M.P.
Pratipaksh, 6/105, Kaushalya Park, Hauz Khas, New Delhi 110016.
Purugrah, Bharat Bhawan, Bhopal, M.P.
Samkaleen Bharatiya Sahitya, Sahitya Akademi, New Delhi.
Sukshatkar, Madhya Pradesh Sahitya Kala Parishad, Professors' Colony, Bhopal, M.P.

Kannada

Lankesh Patrika, Bangalore, Karnataka 560002.
Sudha, Bangalore, Karnataka.
Shankramana, Dharwar, Karnataka 580001.
Tushara, Manipal, Karnataka 576119.

Malayalam

Mathrubhumi, Cherootty Road, Calicut 673001.
Kalakaumudi, Kalakaumudi Publications Pvt. Ltd., Pettah, Thiruvananthapuram 695024.
Katha, Kaumudi Building, Pettah, Thiruvananthapuram 695024.
Kairalisudha, Thrissur.
Malayalaya Manorama, Malayala Manorama Co. Ltd., Post Box 26, Kottayam 686001.
Janayugam, Janayugam Publications Ltd., Kodappakada, Kollam 691001.
Kumkumam, Lakshminand, Kollam 691001.
Bhasha Poshini, Malayala Manorama Co. Ltd., Kottayam 686001.
Kerala Kaumudi, Post Box 77, Trivandrum
Manorayyam, Manorayyam Press, T.B. Junction, Kottayam 686001.

Marathi

Anushtubh, Maharastra Sahitya Parishad, Tilak Road, Pune 411030.
Gulmohar, S.K. Belwalkar Publishing Co., 1347 Sadashivpet, Kamalabai Bhat Marg, Pune 411030.

Mouj, Khatanwadi, Girgaon, Bombay 400004.

Tamil

Amudha Surabhi, 123, Angappa Naicken St., Madras 600001.
Ananda Vikatan, Vasan Publications Pvt. Ltd., 151, Mount Road, Madras 600002.
Dinamani Kadir, C V Raman Express Estate, Mount Road, Madras 600002.
Kalki, Barastham Publications, 84/1-6, Race Course Road, Guindy, Madras 600032.
Kalaimagal, 1, Sanskrit College Street, Madras 600004.
Kanaiyazhi, 149, Bells Road, Madras 600024.
Kumudam, 83, Purasawakkam High Road, Madras 600010
Ponmagal, 6-A, Karnekar Street, Vadapalani, Madras 600026.
India Today (Tamil Edition), A1/A2 Second Floor, Gemini Parsn Commercial Complex, Kodambakkam High Road, Madras 600006.

Telugu

Andhra Prabha Illustrated Weekly Andhraprabha Pvt. Ltd., Express Centre, Domal Guda, Hyderabad 500029.
Andhra Jyothi Sachitra Vara Patrika, Chetla Bazar, Vijayawada 520002
Andhra Patrika, 14/4/21, Mallikarjunar Street, Gandhinagar, Vijayawada 520002.
Swati, Prakasam Road, Governorpet, Vijayawada 520001.
Pragathi Sachitra Vara Patrika, Visalandhra Buildings, Machavaram Post, Vijayawada 520001.
Racchabanda, Jammikunta, Tg. Huzurabad, Dist. Karimnagar 505001.

Urdu

Shabkhoon, 313 Rani Mandi, Allahabad.
Asri Adab, D-7, Model Town, Delhi 110009.
Qaumi Zaban, Anjuman Tarraqi Urdu (Pakistan) Baba-i-Urdu Road, Karachi 1, Pakistan.
Shair, Muktaba Qasr-ul-Adab, Bombay Central Post Office, Post Box No. 4526, Bombay 400008.
Naya Daur, Post Box No. 146, Lucknow.

Aajkal, Publication Division, Patiala House, New Delhi.
Kitab Numa, Maktaba Jamia Ltd., Jamia Nagar, New Delhi 110025.
Zehn-e-Jadeed, Post Box No. 7042, New Delhi 110002.
Aaj, B—140, Sector 11 B, North Karachi Township, Karachi, Pakistan.

N.B. This is by no means an exhaustive list of all the contemporary journals, periodicals, newspapers (the magazine sections), little magazines and anthologies which give space to the short story. For the most part, these names represent the range of publications consulted by the nominating editors in their respective languages. However, since the compilation of a far more detailed list of publications is one of KATHA VILASAM's objectives, the editors would welcome any additional information on the subject, particularly with respect to languages not covered in this volume.